STORIES BY EGYPTIAN WOMEN

STORIES BY EGYPTIAN WOMEN

My Grandmother's Cactus

Introduced and translated
by Marilyn Booth

UNIVERSITY OF TEXAS PRESS
AUSTIN

First published by Quartet Books Limited 1991
A member of the Namara Group
as *My Grandmother's Cactus: Stories by Egyptian Women*

Translation copyright © 1991 by Marilyn Booth
All rights reserved
Printed in the United States of America

First University of Texas Press edition, 1993
Published by arrangement with Quartet Books Limited

Library of Congress Cataloging-in-Publication Data

Stories by Egyptian women : my grandmother's cactus /
introduced and translated by Marilyn Booth. —
1st University of Texas Press ed.
p.   cm.
Originally published in Great Britain under title:
My grandmother's cactus.
ISBN 0-292-70803-3 (pbk. : alk. paper)
1. Short stories, Arabic—Egypt—Translations into
English.   2. Short stories, Arabic—Women authors—
Translations into English.   3. Arabic fiction—20th century—
Translations into English.   I. Booth, Marilyn.   II. Title:
My grandmother's cactus.
PJ8216.S76   1993
892'.7301089287—dc20   92-43065

CONTENTS

Preface and Acknowledgements

In translating these stories, I have tried to convey the very different styles and approaches of their writers. Because the stories are full of contextual references and specific socially meaningful gestures and phrases, they carry footnotes which I hope will be helpful rather than intrusive.

Several individuals have contributed to this book in one way or another. I want to thank Margot Badran, Kenneth Cuno, Angeline Eichhorst, Ferial Ghazoul, Edwar al-Kharrat, Denys Johnson-Davies and Djuke Poppinga for their suggestions and support, and Suzanne Masoud and Wahid Sami for reading certain translations and giving me the benefit of their linguistic knowledge and literary sensibilities.

But most of all, I feel gratitude to the authors represented in this collection. All of the writers have participated in this project, some reading the final translations of their stories, others discussing specific points. This book is in more than one way a joint effort, which has made it particularly rewarding. And perhaps most gratifying of all are the new friendships that have resulted.

Biographies of Authors

Radwa Ashour was born in Cairo in 1946 and grew up in that city. In addition to fiction, her writings include critical studies of Palestinian and West African writers and an account of her experiences as a post-graduate student in the US. Her second novel and a volume of short stories have just been published, and she is currently working on a play. She is married to the Palestinian poet Murid al-Barghuti and they have one son.

Salwa Bakr was born in Cairo 'about forty years ago'. She began writing short stories in the early 1970s and has had them published in many journals and in three collections of her own work. Her studies at Ain Shams University, Cairo, have included business studies, theatre criticism and history. She lives in a new suburb of Cairo on the edge of the desert with her artist husband and small daughter.

Seham Bayomi was born in Cairo in 1949. She has moved from social work to journalism and works for the newspaper *al-Jumhuriyya*. She first published short stories in the early 1970s and her stories have appeared in literary publications throughout the Arab world; her second collection is to be published shortly and she is at present working on her first novel.

Neamat al-Biheiri was born in 1953. A qualified accountant, she began writing in 1980 when 'a memorable encounter with a would-be suitor'gave her an idea for a story ('Half a Woman'). She has published in several literary journals and has brought out two collections of her own work. She lives with her writer-husband in the Cairo suburb of Madinat Nasr, which provides the setting for one of her stories published here, 'The Way to the Seventh'.

Etidal Osman was born in Cairo in 1942 but spent her first five years in the Delta province of al-Qalyubiyya. That experience runs through many of her stories. In addition to being a fiction writer and critic, she is managing editor of the literary journal *Fusul*. She 'always dreamed of writing' and wrote a lot as a teenager. Her first published story, 'The Day the Madness Stopped', is to be found in this collection. She has a book of critical essays as well as a collection of short stories in print and is interested in experimenting with different forms. She is married and has two sons.

Mona Ragab was born in Cairo in 1953. She studied economics and political science at Cairo University and is currently cultural deputy editor of the newspaper *al-Ahram*. She began writing poetry and short stories at school, and has had many short stories published in *al-Ahram*. Her first collection appeared in 1985 and a second is to be available shortly. She is working on a novel which she hopes to publish in the coming year. She is married and has a teenage daughter and a younger son.

Ibtihal Salem was born in Cairo in 1949. She attended a French *lycée* and took a degree in psychology at Ain Shams University, Cairo. Leaving Cairo to live with her husband in Port Said, she found that the magical world of the sea and the vitality of everyday life in that city and port had a great influence on her short stories. She returned to Cairo after ten years, where she works as a translator for state radio and television and in one of the public-sector theatres. She has published numerous stories in magazines and has received several certificates of recognition from cultural institutions in Egypt. Her first collection of stories was published recently and a second one is in preparation. She lives in Cairo with her teenage son.

Sahar Tawfiq was born in Cairo in 1951 and is a school-teacher by profession. She began writing at the age of nine and has been writing ever since. Her first story was published in 1972 and subsequently a collection of her stories appeared. Her writings have appeared in literary journals in Egypt and elsewhere in the Arab world. She continues to write and lives with her sculptor-husband Adel al-Sharqawi and their two young sons near the Pyramids – where until a few years ago they were surrounded by fields.

Glossary: Terms of Address

Amm: 'paternal uncle'; by extension, a term of address for older men one considers as uncles and, more generally, for older men of the neighbourhood who are perceived as members of one's own or a lower social class.

Effendi: a title, now obsolete, reserved for men of the middle classes with some education, such as civil servants and, more specifically, schoolteachers.

Khala: 'maternal aunt', more generally 'auntie'; a somewhat familiar-affectionate, but still respectful form of address for an older woman whom one doesn't necessarily know personally.

Sitt: a respectful form of address for a married woman or an older woman or for one's grandmother; *sitti*: 'my grandmother'.

INTRODUCTION

This collection presents eight short-story writers of Egypt. Born in the 40s or early 50s, they are a new generation of women writers whose work began to emerge in the late 70s and early 80s. Like their male contemporaries, they are exploring new literary structures, linguistic and symbolic fields and themes. Some are trying to break down traditional genre boundaries; some are exploring the specifically Arabic, and Egyptian, heritages of narrative and tradition, returning to historic moments and mythological presences in their own culture and reshaping them.

Traditionally, Arab women's varied historical experiences have generated literary expression mostly from 'outside' – that is, from the points of view of men writers. Yet, however silenced or marginalized, however 'spoken-for', women have had their literary voices throughout the history of Arabic culture. Since pre-Islamic times individual women have received recognition for literary excellence, while women as bearers of oral culture have been central to preserving and continually reshaping traditional expressive forms. Women writers in Egypt today, while part of a flourishing contemporary Arabic literary culture, are conscious both of their minority representation in cultural production (and the social marginalization underlying that) and of their 'grandmothers', of a tradition of Arab women writing. They are aware of the different perspectives that women may bring to literary composition and, in that light, they read their 'grandmothers'.

Aware of tradition, these writers are also markedly different from earlier generations of women writers in

Egypt – a difference which might be illustrated by the history of the short story in Egypt.[1]

Women Writers and the History of the Short Story in Egypt

The non-official press and non-governmental book-publishing sector were firmly established in Egypt by the late nineteenth century; and ever since, women have contributed consistently to both, albeit in much smaller numbers than their male counterparts. Educated at home by parents or tutors, women of Middle Eastern élites could hone their literary skills while still abiding by the strict limitations on physical and social movement marking the lives of upper-class women into the early twentieth century. They could move beyond those boundaries by publishing their writings. Women wrote on a wide range of issues but focused especially on women's experiences, needs and due rights. Some turn-of-the-century women writers also tried to find common ground with women from other economic strata, for whom need dictated a physical presence in the public sphere.

Women in late-nineteenth-century Egypt, like men, published mostly non-fiction and poetry. But the development of an audience and market for fiction encouraged women to use new forms. Although medieval Arabic literature had its narrative genres, the novel and short-story forms were in the first instance direct imports from the West, brought back by intellectuals who travelled to Europe and also taken up by those who, remaining in the Arab world, had close contacts with European culture. Readings, translations and adaptations of European and American fiction generated experimentation in the new forms in the late nineteenth century. Original works and 'arabizations' of fiction from other literatures (usually loose translations adapted for Egyptian readers) appeared side by side in the Arabic press and on bookstands. Historical novels flourished, for their instructive possibilities made them both respectable and useful. In the early twentieth century, with the rise of organized nationalism and the struggle against imperialist control, writers turned their attention more fully and explicitly to their own time and place, generating a fictional realism focusing on what they saw as central public issues, 'the woman question' among them.

Beginning in the 1890s, periodicals focusing specifically on 'women's issues' and directed at a female audience were founded, mostly by women, many of whom were immigrants from provinces of the western Fertile Crescent. Part of the emerging feminist debate, these publications tackled issues such as women's access to education, employment and political participation. At the same time, they focused on home management, childbearing and marriage relations. They gave women a forum for contributing to public discussion and a context for developing their writing. Women contributed essays, studies and poetry to magazines such as *The Young Woman* (founded in 1892), *Young Woman of the East* (founded in 1906), *The Fair Sex* (founded in 1908), *The Magazine of the Egyptian Woman* (founded in 1920), *The Magazine of the Women's Awakening* (founded in 1921), *Hope* (founded in 1922) and others.

While fiction was rarely published in these magazines, there did appear transitional forms such as the 'story-essay' in which the fictional or quasi-fictional presentations of characters and situations do not stand on their own but are interwoven with expository prose; the 'story' elements support the central point of the essay.[2] For example, in the fourth volume (1901) of the women's magazine *Anis al-Jalis* we find a 'story-essay' by Labiba Hashim (1880-1947), a Lebanese immigrant to Egypt who founded the long-running magazine *Young Woman of the East* five years later. Entitled 'Woman's Heart', Hashim's contribution to the earlier publication begins with a description of a young woman in a metaphoric garden and follows her through the seasons of her life from hope to disappointment, narrating her meeting and unfolding relationship with the 'man of her dreams'. This precedes a short homily on the importance of knowledge, mutual consideration and spiritual nourishment in a happy marital relationship.[3]

Hashim was also an early experimenter in the composition of short fiction that would stand independent of expository support. As one literary historian has noted, however, her original stories 'were not so fortunate as to attract the attention of historians of modern literature'. Though ignored by critics, these stories did place her in the ranks of men writers of the time who were also experimenting with fiction.[4] Hashim and other women also tried their hand at 'arabizations' of European stories.

Women also wrote longer fiction – the poet 'Aisha al-Taymuriyya (1840–1902) published a long allegorical tale in 1887/8 – and also plays, but the short story seems to have held the limelight.[5] In general, the literati of turn-of-the-century Egypt did not 'specialize' in one genre; and in this women writers were no exception.[6] Although their most noticeable vehicle was the periodical press, they published books as well. The numbers are low, though, in the context of the enormous publishing output in Egypt: from 1900 to 1925, at least sixty-two volumes in Arabic authored, translated or compiled by thirty-one Arab women were published.[7] These include nine novels and novellas by seven women writers, plus four works of European fiction translated into Arabic by women. They also include several collections of prose poetry and 'story-essays', notably by Mayy Ziyada (1886–1941), another immigrant from Ottoman Syria who gained renown in Egyptian literary circles, her career as writer, translator, public speaker and feminist publicist spanning the years 1911–35.

The short story, easier to publish in periodicals and able to present discrete and concrete issues and to convey pithy messages, flourished in Egypt from the early 1920s on. Women writers tended to focus more on the short story as their men colleagues concentrated increasingly on the novel.[8] This may be partly because short-story writing could more easily be fitted in with other demands made on women's lives (contemporary women writers mention this factor!). And there was the attraction of the short story as a vehicle for social and political comment, addressing issues of women's rights and needs among other subjects.

A good example is to be found in *The Egyptian Woman*, founded by the Egyptian Feminist Union in 1937. Its first editor-in-chief, Fatima Ni'mat Rashid, published one of her own short stories in the fifth issue. 'In the Moonlight: the Blossoming Sant Trees'[9] tells the story of a young and unschooled peasant girl who develops a friendship with the son of a wealthy landowner; but their relationship, in the context of class differences and the girl's dependent ignorance, can only lead to *her* death. Published during the heyday of literary romanticism in Egypt, this story with its feverish heroine, her 'burial shroud' of petals, the simple, grieving father and the young 'hero' on horseback, seems far from social criticism in the Egyptian context. But it does express issues of salience at the time: the relationship between city and village, the absentee landlord's wealth contrasted with the condition of the peasantry as the 'backbone' of Egyptian society, the effects accruing from the failure to educate girls – issues of class, gender and national strength combined. Formulaic and romantic as it strikes us now, the tale weaves major concerns of the time into fictional form for the upper- and middle-class readers of *The Egyptian Woman*.

From Periodicals to Collections

The earliest published volume of short stories in Arabic by an Egyptian woman appeared in 1935, two decades

after the earliest collections of stories by men writers in
Egypt. Suhayr al-Qalamawi (born 1911), who has since
had a distinguished career as a scholar and professor of
Arabic literature, published *My Grandmother's Tales* two
years before becoming the first woman to receive an MA
in Arabic literature from the Egyptian (now Cairo)
University.[10] The title of the present collection, while
drawn from one of the stories translated here, echoes this
earlier, key collection. Taking the form of an elderly
woman's memories told to her granddaughter, al-
Qalamawi's tales seem to echo a medieval Arabic
structure, setting stories within a framework of a single
narrator-auditor pair. Dwelling on the past through the
filter of the grandmother's memory, the book also takes
up contemporary issues through the generation gap
revealed in the pair's conversations, in their friendly
disagreements – elucidating the enormous range of
possibilities which middle-class girls enjoyed in the
Egypt of the 1930s as compared to fifty years before. As
the critic Hilary Kilpatrick has noted, 'In this book a
woman plays her traditional role of storyteller and
historical memory.'[11] The historical memory of *My
Grandmother's Tales* places emphasis less on public events
than on the lives of those who, for example, stayed at
home in wartime; the focus is on a woman's world.

While contemporaries of al-Qalamawi began to
publish their own collections of short stories in the early
1940s, in the early 1950s the number of women publishing short stories increased markedly. Most of the writers
of this generation had full-time professional careers;
many worked as journalists. Gadhibiyya Sidqi, Ihsan
Kamal, Amina al-Sa'id, Zaynab Sadiq, Asma' Halim,
Sufi 'Abdallah, Malik 'Abd al-'Aziz and others have
portrayed women's lives in a realist vein, describing
them as shaped and usually constrained by the rigid
social expectations surrounding home management and
childbearing in marriage as women's prescribed roles.
Professional goals, if any, are seen to create conflicting

demands on women in a rapidly changing but socially rigid context. The trajectories that their female characters know are familiar ones: desires thwarted, independence crushed, achievements scorned. Many stories mount critiques of polygamy, men's right to immediate divorce and parental power to choose their daughters' husbands. While both women and men are seen as victims of such practices, women are presented as the more powerless and thus the more victimized. Often, the stories of this period are explicitly didactic, bearing a clear 'moral'; sometimes they degenerate into triteness and sentimentality. But increasingly, social and political messages are more finely incorporated into the fictional world. Some women writers have concentrated on their own middle-class, usually urban milieux; others, like Asma' Halim, have attempted to portray girls and women marginalized by class as well as by gender.

Many of these stories written in the 1950s invite feminist readings. They suggest that the traditional confines of female experience ill-prepare women to organize and sustain new kinds of lives that are, at least in name, becoming possible. But it was in the 1960s and 1970s that fiction by women began to express feminist concerns and goals more explicitly and boldly. As an example, Nawal al-Saadawi, controversial for her non-fiction works on the control of women's sexuality in Arab societies, especially the landmark *Woman and Sex* (1972), had already begun to express her concerns through fiction in an early short-story collection, *I Learnt Love* (1959). In the first story we meet an urban, highly educated, professional woman encountering peasant society and having to come to terms with her own preconceived notions. The author attempts a forthright treatment of class, gender and urban-rural divides. Since then, al-Saadawi has published many short stories as well as novels and non-fiction works. Her fiction drama-tizes the control of sexuality and 'honour' in a patriarchal society and the manifestations that oppression against women take. The didactic dimensions of al-Saadawi's activism are clear in her short stories and novels; hers is not the only contemporary Arabic feminist-oriented fiction in which the primacy of the message dominates, but it is the most renowned.

Other dimensions of feminist concern begin to surface in the works of writers who emerged in the 1960s and 1970s. Alifa Rifaat, who began to publish stories in the 1950s but then was kept from writing and publishing for over a decade by her husband's opposition, puts forward the claim that a married woman has the basic right to a fully satisfying sexual and emotional life.[12] Her boldness in presenting women's sexual desires is still unusual. When Iqbal Baraka, a journalist, began writing fiction, she was motivated in part by pressures which she herself faced as a young woman and saw in the lives of other Egyptian women.[13] Sikkina Fuad's concern with images of women in society achieved an audience broader than that for published fiction when her novella *The Day Fatima was Arrested* was adapted for radio and cinema. Latifa al-Zayyat, a university professor of English and comparative literature, has not only written important works of fiction but has also investigated the women characters in fiction by contemporary Arab men writers in a recent study (*Some Images of Women in Arabic Short Stories and Novels*, 1989). Her novel *The Open Door* (1960) explored political and metaphorical links between women's lives and the national struggle for liberation; her short story collection *Old Age and Other Stories* (1986) reflects on social contradictions particularly as they are embodied in women's experiences, and she experiments by drawing on, for example, the diary form.

A New Generation

Not many Egyptian women writers of fiction have been translated into English but most anthologies of Arabic short stories in English translation do include one or two

by women writers,[14] while Nawal al-Saadawi and Alifa
Rifaat have become well known in the English speaking
world through translations of books of their own. This
volume represents the first collection in English translation of short stories by Egyptian women writers.

This collection presents only a few of the many
women writing short stories today in Egypt. In the first
instance, it represents a personal and individual choice
of stories I have found particularly intriguing. The
project began as an anthology in the more usual sense: a
collection of stories which would include a sweeping
range of short fiction by women in Egypt from the 1940s
to the present. As my choices came to centre on new
writers, I decided to focus entirely on them and to offer
more than one story by each one chosen, thus giving
readers an opportunity to acquaint themselves a bit
more with each writer than is possible in the traditional
anthology.

At the same time, I have tried to present a wide
variety. That is not hard to do: these writers are all
moving in different directions, writing in their own
distinctive styles, pursuing their separate - if inter-
related - interests. Nor is it difficult in most cases to
choose stories which may indicate each writer's breadth
of technique and concern.

Thus, this collection should not be seen in terms of any
across-the-board representation of women writing and
publishing short stories in Egypt. But it is worth noting
that these women are all receiving the recognition of
serious critical treatment. Their importance is recognized by contemporary Arab scholars, whether in the
form of written studies, papers delivered at conferences
and seminars or critical sessions focusing on individual
works at Cairo's Atelier, a forum for writers, artists and
critics. Moreover, these writers are self-critical, eager for
serious appraisal.

These women writers are part of a generation which
has to a great extent broken away from traditional

realist modes of expression. Their revolt hinges on a concept of reality which privileges the changing, the uncertain and the fragmented over the stable, the controllable and the unified. It is linked also to an understanding of the complex historical and class dimensions of individual identities – both women's and men's; to a refusal to see women's control over their own lives as dependent on men's good will; and to a rejection of the notion of essentialist definitions of 'male' and 'female'.

These writers are experimenting with language in ways that incorporate 'the silenced side' of society, 'the marginalized half, those deliberately ignored'[15] into the fictional world. In fact, they put the silenced at the centre. Salwa Bakr explores the complex links between everyday spoken usage and the 'traditional' language of written literature – for there exists a wider gulf between the two than is true in contemporary English. She finds the origins of colloquial phrases in the literary heritage and shapes them into her own lexicon, dramatizing her protagonists' thought patterns, producing humorous effects through socio-linguistic ironies. In Bakr's 'Zeenat Marches in the President's Funeral', the external world of politics is rearranged in the protagonist's own logic and language as she fills out her everyday world for the reader. Neamat el-Biheiry experiments with the use of colloquial proverbs, metaphors and dialogue to colour her fictional world as defined by female protagonists of an economically and politically marginalized sector of the urban populace. Ibtihal Salem moves between a highly compressed, poetic diction, as in 'Smoke Ring', and the detached, external description – even as she enters her protagonist's mind – of 'City of Cardboard'. Etidal Osman is interested in making language itself the main character of her stories – a challenge to the translator! Seham Bayomi's concise diction and spare use of dialogue clash productively with the fantasia-like but joltingly real worlds she creates. Radwa Ashour and Sahar Tawfiq incorporate echoes from the Qur'an into the everyday mental worlds of their stories. Tawfiq undermines the notion of a stable point of view as she switches pronouns on the reader.[16] Ashour experiments with inserting theatre into the short story – in form, not just in content or description. Mona Ragab creates a detached style of externalized narration which will not accept what it describes, as we witness an incident that can only increase the alienation and pressures felt by her protagonist in 'The Day the Chickens Escaped'. Or, we find the ironic reality-unreality of 'The Sleeping City' carrying a new twist on the emperor's 'old' clothes.

These writers are also part of a literary generation that is turning increasingly to its own historical pasts. There is marked interest among these writers in Pharaonic, early Coptic and Islamic motifs, and in how all of them intersect with traditional expressive culture. As noted, both the Qur'an and colloquial proverbs run through these stories; far from being superficial stylistic flourishes, they represent major formative elements in the story worlds portrayed. Other cultural topoi emerge. El-Biheiry draws on the figures of Isis and Osiris, and ancient religious figures are incorporated into today's experience, in the dream-and-everyday lives of their protagonists. Osman draws on traditional tales that children are told, ones that happen to have their parallels in European culture, in the 'Rapunzel' mould. Osman also uses the story of the Prophet Jonah to tell a tale of contemporary village life and the changes wrought by 'development'. Mermaids, djinnis, rituals, celebrations: the historical and the mythological come together in the stories. The Nile becomes a mythic river and a symbolic journey – a source of exploration, new life, and vulnerability and dangers too. Thus, the centrality of the Nile to Egyptian life takes on many layers of significance. All of these writers are based firmly in the present. Old mythologies are part of today's realities.

Women's Lives, Feminist Readings

No longer do women write from seclusion. But their lives and the expectations they must meet create barriers to the practice of their craft; some obstacles they share with their men colleagues, others they don't. As these writers reflect on their craft, they note over and over the factors that impede them, many of which will sound familiar to women the world over. Like most of their male counterparts, they cannot devote themselves wholly to their writing, or at least not to their fictional writing; full-time jobs and financial pressures prevent that. At least four of the eight writers have new stories, novellas or novels currently finished - but they sit in the desk drawer, for the writers can't find time, or child-free space, to copy them out cleanly for the publisher. Women in particular cannot always get away to attend functions of concern to them as writers - for example, the Tuesday-night literary seminars at the Cairo Atelier. Women may face early family discouragement of a writing career, difficulties in finding publishing outlets and the dismissive reactions of critics - especially as there are relatively few women (not to mention feminist) critics focusing on contemporary literature. Some of these writers feel they've 'started late' because of various obstacles, whether those of career pressures or family. In addition, women writers in particular may face a struggle against self-censorship as their writings tend to be taken - more than those of men are - as transparently autobiographical. What readers have wanted from women writers are 'true confessions'.[17] The fact that women have been less represented in published literature in Arabic means that some women feel they write, if not in a literary vacuum, then in a new and relatively untrampled space - a proposition they may find at once depressing, daunting, exciting and liberating.

These writers are all Cairenes, which reflects the heavy concentration of cultural activity that has marked

Egypt's capital throughout this century. As is true of so much earlier and contemporary literature in Arabic, The City (or a certain part of it) becomes a repository of varying values, experiences and kinds of change, and a sort of transition point between Egypt and political, economic and social intrusions from outside. The particular historical-social situation of provincial cities emerges in Ibtihal Salem's stories, coloured by her own long experience in the commercial port and wartime front line of Port Said. And encounters between different Cairos, equally telling, come out in a number of stories. But the writers' urban backgrounds do not cause them to focus exclusively on the urban scene. Like many earlier writers, women and men, they concern themselves with Egypt's wider, agricultural and provincial, world. Links – and distances – between city life and various rural ecologies and societies (the agricultural Delta, Upper Egypt, sparsely settled but quickly 'developing' sea-coast areas) mark Ashour's two stories, Osman's 'Jonah of the Sea', Bayomi's 'The Sea Knows' and El-Biheiry's 'The Way to the Seventh'.

Women's lives and perspectives are at the centre of many of these stories – which *is* representative with regard to both earlier and contemporary women's fiction writing in Egypt. And being a woman is equated with having an unequal share – materially, spatially, socially and ideologically. Even if the writers would not privilege feminist readings of their stories, it is not hard to find feminist perspectives in the texts. Yet this focus serves to highlight marginality, violence and oppression as marking both the gender position of 'woman' and the class position of those, both women and men, who have been deprived of power by economic and political structures and processes. Thus, in Salwa Bakr's stories, female characters are often 'social misfits', existing at the margins, representing that which will not be incorporated as 'normal' by the dominant, official ideology. And this emerges in the use of names: those of female characters are often either mispronounced, unknown or unsaid in her stories. While oppressive and marginalizing social relations are at the centre of works by certain men writers of the same 'generation', it is in these women's writings that the combined effects of class and gender in marginalizing large numbers of Egyptians become central, as do struggles for communication and understanding as bases for transforming consciousness and hence experience.

This writing generation has come to literary maturity in a period of rapid and shocking change in Egypt and the Arab world as a whole. The authors in this book were aged between fourteen and twenty-five when the June 1967 War, and defeat at the hands of the Israelis, struck a devastating emotional and intellectual blow to the Egyptian, and wider Arab, intelligentsia that had embraced the socialism of Gamal Abd el-Nasser. They were a few years older when the changing direction of Egyptian economic policy was enshrined in Anwar el-Sadat's Open Door Policy, with its uncritical embrace of Western capitalist enterprise and political alliance. The consequences of that reorientation, as well as ongoing problems which remain unsolved, are becming ever clearer in Egypt today, inscribed in a rampant consumerism, high inflation, increased overcrowding and pollution and economic pressures to cancel subsidies on basic goods. As boutiques with English and French names spring up and Mercedes sedans crowd the streets, buying vegetables – let alone meat – becomes an impossibility for the majority. Many people take on two jobs; many try to emigrate. These and other constants of life for most Egyptians today run throughout stories by the writers in this book, who are anything but isolated, either in their lives or in their writings, from contemporary life in Egypt.

Marilyn Booth
Cairo
March 1990

NOTES

1. For an overview of women writers in modern Arabic literature, see Hilary Kilpatrick, 'Women and Literature in the Arab World: The Arab East', pp. 72–90 in Mineke Schipper (ed), *Unheard Words: Women and Literature in Africa, the Arab World, Asia, the Caribbean and Latin America*, translated by Barbara P. Fasting, Allison and Busby, London 1985.

2. See Yusuf al-Sharuni (ed), *Al-layla al-thaniyya ba'da ul-ulf*, GEBO, Cairo 1975, editor's introduction, pp. 9–10.

3. Labiba Hashim (Madi), 'Qalb al-mar'a', *Anis al-jalis*, vol. 4, no. 12, 31 Dec. 1901, pp. 888–92.

4. Anwar al-Jundi, *Adab al-mar'a al-'arabiyya: tatawwuruhu wa-a'lamuhu*, Matba'at al-Risala, Cairo. n.d., p. 42.

5. 'Aisha 'Ismat al-Taymuriyya, *Nata'ij al-ahwal fi al-aqwal wa'l-af'al* (*The Results of Circumstances in Words and Deeds*), Cairo 1305 AH (1887/8). See my translation of the opening pages in M. Badran and M. Cooke (eds), *Opening the Gates: A Century of Arab Feminist Writing*, Virago, London 1990. Zaynab Fawwaz (1845–1914), contributor to many periodicals and a fiction writer, wrote the play *Passion and Fidelity* (*Riwayat al-Hawa wa'l-wafa'*), al-Matba'a al-Jami'a, Cairo 1310 AH (1892/3). Alexandra Khouri Avierino, founder of *Anis al-Jalis* and like Fawwaz an immigrant from greater Syria, published a play and 'arabized' French works of fiction (al-Jundi, op. cit., p. 37).

6. Al-Sharuni, op. cit., p. 10, makes this point with regard to women writers of the 1930s.

7. I have computed these figures from Ayda Ibrahim Nusayr, *Al-Kutub al-'arabiyya allati nushirat fi Misr 1900–1925*, American University in Cairo Press, Cairo 1983.

8. Hilary Kilpatrick makes this point ('Women and Literature', p. 79).

9. Fatima Ni'mat Rashid, 'Fi daw' al-qamar: ashjar

al-sant al-zahira', *al-Misriyya*, vol. 1, no. 5, 15 April 1937, pp. 36–9.

10. The early feminist magazine *al-Misriyya* (*The Egyptian Woman*) celebrated this event as a milestone and a beginning. See *al-Misriyya*, vol. 1, no. 4, 15 March 1937, p. 38.

11. Kilpatrick, p. 80.

12. See Alifa Rifaat, *Distant View of a Minaret and Other Stories*, translated by Denys Johnson-Davies, Quartet Books, London 1983.

13. Comments made by Iqbal Baraka during the conference-workshop on 'Identity in Literature by Women: Egypt and Germany', Goethe Institute, Cairo, 12–13 October 1986.

14. A happy exception is the recent collection selected and translated by William Hutchinson, *Egyptian Tales and Short Stories of the 1970s and 1980s*, American University in Cairo Press, Cairo 1987.

15. Etidal Osman, characterizing a central focus of today's young women writers in Egypt, in her paper 'al-Fatat al-Misriyya wa'l-kitaba al-adabiyya' ('The Young Egyptian Woman and Literary Composition'), presented at a seminar organized by the Arab Women's Solidarity Association, Cairo, 3 October 1987, p. 2.

16. Osman points to this in the paper cited above.

17. This is also noted by al-Sharuni, pp. 14–15, and Kilpatrick, p. 88.

WOMAN ON THE GRASS

Salwa Bakr

Complicity (handwritten annotation)

The Woman, the Boy and the Dog

From among the tombs, where the living reside above the dead,* came the woman, mother of the boy who is master of the dog.

Carrying her shallow white metal bowl, rusted around the rim and full of yellow lupine beans, she swept her eyes across the expanse of ground to select a grassy patch good enough to settle on, one which would provide the best possible position for sighting customers. The boy, her son, wearing the remains of shoes wide enough to accommodate another foot next to each of his own, began to study a swarm of ants who had formed a funeral procession for a small beetle. The third member of the trio, their dog, twisted his head upward, sniffing at the breeze and setting his gaze protestingly on a kite circling in the sky that carried a small bird between its claws.

The woman sat down on a rise of ground, beneath a tree which had clothed the earth with its falling autumn leaves, and whispered to herself after a gust of cold wind had pierced her to the bones:

'First warnings of winter.'

The Seasoned Detective is Preoccupied with His Work

From the other side of the road – which separates the
city of the living from that of the dead – came the
seasoned detective, striding over the grass, now putting
his hand in his pocket, now twirling his moustache, his
eyes never straying from the ground, all the while
emitting long, angry snorts from his nostrils. He was
thinking in some confusion: how and where could he
come up with five cases for the officer within three days?

'Five jobs in three days?' An inner voice echoed the
words in rancour. Two prostitution, one begging and
the rest miscellaneous?

'What sort of old bat could have produced such a
bastard?' he asked himself. 'And what am I supposed to
do? Pull cases out of a hat? He means to get himself a new
star to shine on his shoulder, whatever the cost? And at
my expense?'

Spitting out a long stream of saliva which he worked
vigorously into the ground with a thick sole, he picked
up his train of thought: begging and miscellaneous, that
will solve it by God's leave. Sometime between today
and tomorrow a quarrel is bound to break out somewhere . . . maybe among the gamblers in al-Asyuti's
coffee house or the doped-up customers at al-Samaluti's
den. He resolved to himself that he would go to both
places after nightfall, and likewise would pass by the
Syrian's bar: something would come up for sure.

The seasoned detective also told himself: 'The son of a
bitch knows that these days in Darrasa* prostitution's
as hard to find as green leaves.' He spat again, cursing
the girls of Darrasa, who had emigrated to other,
richer, areas of the city – Agouza, Muhandiseen – and
to the foreigners and those Gulf Arabs and furnished
flats.

The wind came up and he raised the collar of his
rough overcoat until its edges brushed his ears. He thrust
one hand in his pocket, searching for the chunk. When

he felt the rustle of the cellophane between his fingers, he went on.

The Seasoned Detective Chats with the Woman, Mother of the Boy

As he approached her station on the grass, he let out his breath with the relief of one who has made a find. He wished her a good evening, and she responded with a wary smile.

Just then the sun was retreating, bound for the horizon, leaving a remnant of its light alone there to transform all creatures into ghostly shapes, warning of the beginnings of evening. A danger signal pulsed like a siren through the veins of the one sitting on the grass. It showed in the tone of her voice when she returned the detective's evening greeting. The seasoned detective rolled his cigarette slowly, meticulously, after biting the chunk into tiny pieces and mixing them with the cigarette tobacco. He lit up. His eyes followed the passage of the flame on the matchstick between his fingers until it went out and he tossed it away.

He inhaled several long draws, distributing them to chest and throat, expelling them from his nostrils into the spacious emptiness. As he handed her the cigarette he intoned another 'good evening', this time long and drawn-out.*

In the bosom of the woman, mother of the boy, the apprehension grew as she drew small, staccato puffs from between her thin lips and asked herself: 'Does such a man bring good?' The smoke had begun to charge her spirits, and she opened her eyes to their widest, until the black irises came closer together and the large bridge of her nose took on the appearance of a partition wall dividing them.

'Aah, if only she weren't . . . squint-eyed. . . .,' said the seasoned detective to himself. 'And so yellowish . . . then I could have wrapped up the prostitution part with her . . . But this cock-teaser, why doesn't she fatten herself up a bit? She couldn't possibly do for prostitution in her present condition. That so-and-so sitting at his desk won't be convinced by her. She's not capable of satisfying anybody's longings, or quenching anybody's thirst. . . . Begging it is . . . and I'm in God's hands.'

Meanwhile she had busied herself with scurrying after a yellow leaf thrust down on the sparse grass and pulled far away by the breeze. She returned to her spot and began shaping the leaf into a new cornet which she added to her others. Another thought came to her.

'Aah, if only I had a man like this "sarge" . . . who would come home bringing his salary at the start of every month . . . I'd give 'im nine kids. One would come out a merchant, another a plumber and then a sharp-shooter, and we'd go on together. I'd stay with him like the women who live in houses do. . . . Chat with the neighbours every morning, cook at noontime, sleep on a comfortable mattress at night. . . .

'But I know why that son of a bitch is coming by right now . . . this time I'll show him what I'm made of!'

As for him – the seasoned detective – he muttered a complaint in her direction from between clamped teeth. He retrieved the cigarette, which was nearly half finished.

'The world's not what it used to be these days, sister, I tell you, not what it used to be. Everything's turned upside down . . . may God provide! Cost of living's going up . . . and that washed-up wretch sitting at his desk in the station, he thinks I've got miracles up my sleeve, thinks I can snatch that star he wants on his shoulder right out of the sky.

'Does that lunatic imagine I can get anywhere near the beggars at Husayn? By God, I can't do that, as long as they pay up regularly and a reasonable amount . . . I'm no low bastard, I don't play dirty, sister, I can't do that.'

He stopped talking and took a last draw on his

cigarette, which had already come to its end and gone
out. He gazed at her; maybe he could catch a glimmer of
what she was thinking. But the black irises, cast always
in the same direction, raised a massive barrier between
him and what was going through her mind. Irritated, he
began rubbing his nose.

Finally, the mother of the boy spoke, in a low voice,
showing the staid composure of a tradeswoman. 'Listen,
now . . . maybe you'll have success, find what you're
looking for. . . .'

The sound of crying interrupted her. The little one
was irritated by the taste of the soft soil which he had
stuffed between his jaws. He began spitting it out, mixed
with his saliva, while she laughed until she was bent
double. She handed him a few lupine beans, saying,
'You son of a so-and-so!'

The seasoned detective put his hand in his pocket,
took out a nougat and tossed it at the boy. Maybe it
would keep him quiet.

'All's well, God willing!' she said, tears flowing from
her eyes from so much laughing.

'All's well, sister!' replied the detective after summon-
ing an artificial smile to his lips. 'If you come along this
time I'll bring you some supper with my very own
hands. Then you'll be in great shape, in the best of states.
Only one night this time, then you'll get out for lack of
firm evidence and our deal will be just like last time. But
supper . . . I'll bring you supper.' He tossed a fifty-piastre
note into her lap.

She had already done her own accounting in her
head. This time around, he wouldn't fool her, wouldn't
cheat her. She would insist on nothing less than a red
headscarf with spangles, and a meat roll from the shop
that sells trotters and tongues.* Now all of this would
cost one twenty-five, plus there were those fifty piastres
already in hand for whatever might come up. She
wouldn't give up the fifty in her hand no matter how
hard he tried – even if he took it back by force. So she

reasoned with herself. To him, she said: 'Bless the
Prophet, Mr Officer, the first time you treated me
unfairly – uh-huh, by God you treated me unfairly! I
won't take it any longer . . . and prices have gone up for
everyone. This time, nothing less than one pound
seventy-five will do. This is fair and right by God's Law.
If you believe and trust in God, now listen: last time I
came back from the barracks, my bones were just about
broken from sleeping on those slabs . . . I can't do it this
time, not unless it's one seventy-five – by my own dear
boy, I can't!'

The detective coughed, pressed his lips together,
crossed his legs, gazed at the lupines and the woman and
the boy and the dog, and wished he could light an
enormous fire and throw them all in, and drag over his
superior officer and put him on top. He frowned and
levelled a piercing look at the woman.

'You've got crafty, Umm Muhammad . . . crafty, by
God, and greed has filled your heart. I told you I'd bring
you supper . . . by God, I'll bring you supper.'

She lowered her head, gazing at the ground, rubbed
her nose with the edge of the black shawl that covered
her head and remained silent for a moment.

'Well, then . . . God grant you success, Mr Officer,
sir,' she said calmly.

The boy laughed in glee as he clambered on to the
dog, pulled it by the tail and shouted at his mother to
look at him. Meanwhile, the detective got up, reached
his hand into his pocket, extracted the pound note,
grabbed the woman's hand and placed the note in her
palm. He closed her fingers tightly around it, saying,
'Tomorrow – we'll meet in the evening.'

The woman looked at the banknote in her hand.
When she had reassured herself that it really was a whole
pound, she whispered, smiling, 'Don't forget to bring
the meat roll with you.'

NOTES

Title note: 'Mar'ah 'ala al-'ushb', from the author's collection *Zeenat fi jinazat al-ra'is*, published privately by the author, Cairo 1986, pp. 7-12.

the tombs, where the living reside above the dead: the City of the Dead, a ring of cemeteries and mausoleums stretching along the old eastern boundaries of Cairo. The tombs are enclosed in small and mostly roofless structures. In them live the tomb caretakers, and many squatters because of the housing shortage in the city; thus the area has become a 'permanent' residential area, but one lacking in most basic amenities.

Darrasa: a densely settled area on the edge of the City of the Dead, part of it merging with the cemeteries. It is the site of some government low-income housing projects.

'good evening', this time long and drawn out: the phrase and usual intonation accompanying the passing on of a hashish cigarette.

the shop that sells trotters and tongues: the *masmat*, a shop-restaurant selling offal and offering sandwiches made with these relatively cheap animal products.

ZEENAT MARCHES IN THE PRESIDENT'S FUNERAL

Salwa Bakr

Her name was supposed to be Zeenat, but everyone called her 'Z'nat'. Even Abduh the Barber, as he finished writing out a letter on her behalf to the President of the Republic – with whom she had persistently and tirelessly corresponded – would wind up what he was writing with the name 'Z'nat Muhammad Ali', after fixing the pen firmly between her fingers, closing his hand over hers and moving both together so that the signature would truly be in her own hand. To make doubly sure, he would moisten the indelible copy pen with his saliva and colour her thumb with it until a dense purple splotch had formed, enough to imprint a clearly distinguishable thumbprint over the letters of her name which they had written together.

One could certainly say that during the final years of the President's life a very special relationship had grown up between him and Zeenat. Yet, although the two of them had never come face to face during that period – and despite everything – it would be difficult to maintain that this was a one-sided relationship. True, they had not met, nor had it ever been feasible for Zeenat to converse with him, to tell him herself, in her own words, all that she wanted to say. Yet the ongoing relationship between them got to the point where she put together a plan: she thought it a detailed one, and absolutely watertight. But the passing of the days, and the hour of implementation, proved its failure – an outcome that had never entered her mind.

Moreover Abduh the Barber rebuked her in no uncertain terms and cautioned her against ever repeating that crazy deed of hers. This time God had shielded her, but it certainly would have been possible for them to have taken her away – to have taken Zeenat, herself – and hidden her beyond the sun,* and even the blue djinnis would have been ignorant of where she dwelt. Abduh went so far as to call her stupid for having imagined that they would allow her even to get near, that near, to the President of the Republic, let alone to attempt to shake his hand – her hand in his – and give him the petition. Furthermore, had she forgotten the soldiers and plainclothesmen and guards, who would be surrounding him on all sides wherever he might go?

If the truth be known, Abduh's advice to Zeenat did no more than belabour the obvious; for Zeenat had experienced at first hand every word he said. Despite the fact that she had concealed herself from the very crack of dawn on the corner of a certain street that she knew the President came along, every Friday after the prayer service . . . despite the fact that she had been able, as a result, to obtain a position at the very front of the crowd that flocked there to greet the President . . . (and this was, by the way, after one of the pupils from the school had written a brief letter which Zeenat intended to submit to the President, just a few quick, short words with no extras. Literally, the text read: 'Z'nat says hallo, and asks what you've done about you-know-what?')

Despite all that, at the moment when she thought the President's car had drawn close enough to allow her to step out across from it, quickly, and rush forward to shake his hand and give him the piece of paper, she was startled to find dozens of rough hands, those of soldiers and other men, shooting out suddenly as if they had dropped from the heavens to fall precisely on her. The hands began pushing her away from the car and the procession so that she fell among feet, many of which (Zeenat noticed at the time) were encased in high leather boots. Against some were fixed pistols enough to butcher an entire town.

But this regrettable incident, and the hideous pains from which Zeenat suffered afterwards, did not prevent her relationship with the President from continuing. Nor did it change her feelings about him one whit. The portraits of him remained exactly where they had always hung in her shack. Those pictures were the sole elements of decor in the hut, which Zeenat had constructed, entirely on her own, out of rocks, mudbrick and tin sheeting, after she had succeeded in taking possession of a few metres of government land bordering the main road. She would sit before it in shifts from early morning until nearly sunset, waiting for the elementary school pupils to come in and out of the school building. It was actually three schools in one, since both girls and boys would go inside, one batch at a time, to have their lessons. Zeenat sold them molasses sticks, popcorn, lupine beans and small plastic toys which then became the happy lot of those who triumphed in games of chance, which they also bought from her.

As for sending the letters to the President, Zeenat did not waver one bit – proof once again that the relationship between her and the President had not been disturbed, and that indeed it remained serene as a summer day. As Zeenat saw it, the incident had taken place behind the President's back; had he been aware that the bastards, those very ones, had prevented her from giving him her salutations, and the piece of paper, then undoubtedly he would have sent them home, somewhere beyond the sun.* For he'd understand, and know Zeenat's good intentions; he'd know that she couldn't possibly mean any harm to him. Otherwise he would not have answered her letters, as he did more than once, nor would her case have undergone consideration by the government, nor would he have sent the woman, an employee of the State, personally to inspect the shack and observe Zeenat's situation and ask her question after question about her state of affairs and how the world was treating her. That official had assured her, indeed, that her case would be dealt with over the next few months.

And the few months immediately following this visit gave Zeenat no reason to feel disappointed in the President. On the contrary, one could safely say that the plan she had sketched out (in the light of clarifications made by the woman from the government) had succeeded this time. Actually, it was a Development Strategy in miniature which Zeenat drew up for herself, its broad outlines encapsulated in the principle that – now and then – she would treat herself to a luxuriously large food intake. In order to activate the project, she would buy a small primus stove and an aluminium pot in which she could cook whenever her insides hankered after meat. She would also undertake to buy a fine corduroy *gallabiyya* and beaded headband to replace the tattered *gallabiyya* that she always wore. And before all else (and by the leave of the One and Only) she would pay back her foreseeable debts, which could be summed up in the two pounds she owed to Abduh the Barber (the final outstanding instalment of an old debt, money she had borrowed from him to buy new goods to trade in). She would also take care of those debts she had not anticipated, consisting of a number of invitations from her brother, the children's father, to eat meat, and several fifty-piastre notes which he had passed on to her at the beginning of each month. Zeenat was determined to visit her brother with two kilos of meat in hand, once she had the money in her grasp. And before all else, a pair of top-notch chickens and a bottle of rosewater-flavoured sherbet, as a sincerely meant gift to Abduh the

Barber which would gladden her own heart, in recognition of the kindliness he had shown her and the service he had performed for her in writing the letters to the President of the Republic. For these were services that finally had been crowned with success, in that it had been stipulated that she would receive an exceptional pension, to the value of three pounds, fully and entirely. Because of those three pounds she had begun to go in person, and in all pride and confidence and esteem for herself and the President of the Republic, to the Government Cashier's Office at the onset of every month, to take receipt of those three pounds after showing the necessary document of exchange, in addition to her identity card. Zeenat was very careful with this card: after it was issued to her, she had preserved it as if it were her own eyes, her most precious possession. There could be no greater proof of this than the fact that she kept the ID in a plastic cover which she had purchased for an entire *shillin* – a whole five-piastre piece. Moreover, she always stuffed the ID away under her mattress for safekeeping, and made sure, every so often, that it was still there. This was not only because of the pension. Once she had been able to stick it full in the eye of a municipality policeman. She had really given it to him, with all self-confidence, when he had tried to pick a quarrel and then fleece her while she was seeing to her own business. He began threatening to drag her to the police station because she had no identity card. Let down, he recoiled – the nape of his neck burning like a hot bread-round – after she had ridiculed and scolded him in strong language.

But the three pounds were not the grand finale of Zeenat's relationship with the President of the Republic. For despite the fact that Zeenat had received a sum of money of which she had never in her whole life dreamt – to the amount of eighteen pounds, since the executive order stipulating her acquisition of the pension had been issued with retroactive force, giving her the right accordingly to claim for the period of six months – and notwithstanding the indisputable fact that she had done wonders with this money – for she had bought some brand-new red bricks with which she finished the walls of the shack, after removing the rocks and tin sheeting, and she had knocked through a window so the breeze and sunlight could enter at their leisure – and had allowed herself a more prosperous lifestyle, so much so that she bought a whole chicken which was an utter delight to eat all by herself, not sharing it with any creature on God's earth . . . an unforgettable delight: that moment when she was steering the boiled flesh, mixed with cooked rice and moistened with its own hot broth, into her mouth . . . despite all of that, and in spite of the fundamental changes which had come into Zeenat's life (among them the increases she managed in the stock of goods in which she dealt, adding new categories, like pencils and erasers) . . . despite all of that, Abduh the Barber – 'May his hands be graced, and may God protect the light of his eyes', as Zeenat, loyal and sincere friend that she was, always said – was constantly advising her to pick up the relationship where it had left off, and to persevere in sending her letters to the President. But, he said, the tone of grievance should be heightened even further, and she should make a specific complaint, asking for an increase in the pension on the basis that she was a helpless woman on her own with no one in the whole wide world to take responsibility for her, and no one to hear and honour her grievances except God and the President of the Republic.

And frankly, Abduh the Barber outdid himself in composing the new missives, surpassing even the strenuous efforts he had made in writing the letters of the first stage. Zeenat's receipt of the pension had been the crowning achievement of that phase, and it had happened because the pertinent law was clear and unequivocal on the question of Zeenat's right to the pension. And, from another perspective, the first letters

had been justified because Zeenat had not yet received
the pension. But now, compliance with a further request
would be in the manner of an exception, and would have
to be based on personal directives from the President of
the Republic, who would be able to issue such an order
once he sensed (by means of the words written to him)
the reality of Zeenat's situation and her difficult
circumstances – for these would melt even a heart of
stone.

Thus, Abduh the Barber massaged his natural talents
vigorously, working to extract the juices of his rhetorical
faculties, trying to have such an effect on the President
that he would issue the decree necessary to raise the
pension. Apparently, though, the standard of what
Abduh wrote was not up to par in one way or another,
for not a single reply arrived from the Presidency
pertaining to the outcome of fully nine letters which
Abduh had written in the presence of Zeenat herself,
and at her direction, on this matter.

Therefore, and just a few days before Zeenat heard
the momentous news, Abduh the Barber had scaled the
heights, reaching his rhetorical summit in the tenth
letter to the President. It cannot be denied that Zeenat
herself had a hand in writing the essential text of this
letter, making exertions that are not open to doubt, after
conferring with Abduh in his little shop for about three
hours, to ensure that the discourse would emerge in the
best possible shape and form. Abduh was obliged to
write it all down several times, after Zeenat had gone on
revising and redrafting the wording, furnishing Abduh
with some new and impressively moving thoughts. The
truth is that Abduh, though indeed a good-natured
chap, could not have borne it so patiently all this time if
it hadn't been the end of the month, when customers
were wanting (for hardly any were putting their feet
inside the door). But Abduh, too, was enjoying himself,
for through writing Zeenat's letters he had discovered
that he could utter passages that had a certain beauty,

ones that were really extremely pleasing and which he himself found most moving – just as the results of his first pieces of writing had really strengthened his confidence in himself and in his great abilities in this sphere. Moreover, he had not forgotten Zeenat's gift to him, which provided a certain encouragement and which was, on the plane of mundane reality, a large male duck which Zeenat had fed (bit by bit, for the space of a week before presenting it to Abduh) dried beans, every evening at suppertime, until it got quite heavy and grew to nearly the size of a pelican. And along with it she had brought two bottles of sherbet, one rosewater and the other apricot. In any case, the gift – in its totality – came as a genuine surprise to Abduh, who had not anticipated that it would be quite this grand and expensive.

For the latest letter, Abduh had tried in the beginning to inject the traditional preamble – which he had written each time, constructing it around expressions of gratitude and praise, and phrases extolling the President of the Republic – with some of his political views concerning the current state of affairs, his opinion of the Americans and the British, the role of feudalism in alliance with colonialist imperialism, and other issues arising from the kind of talk of which Abduh was very fond. He tried to write this preamble in a way that would show the extent of his perusal of the newspapers, and the magazines too. From this beginning, he meant to move on to the subject of Z'nat and her request, ending with her hopes that the President's life be long and that he be graced with blessings, he and his children, as well as with an invoking of God to spare him the evil of his enemies and all their zealous proponents.

But Zeenat, She of the Plans, was carrying around in her head a new concept of how they might frame the discourse, an idea that took shape through her daily sessions before the portraits of the President, as she sat conversing with them. For after his reply to her and after the episode of the three pounds, Zeenat had come to feel a very warm affection for the President of the Republic. She felt that he was her true support in the world, and deep down she sensed that his pictures kept her company, cheering her up in her solitude and removing the dreariness from her soul whenever she was alone in the shack. Thus she decided to talk to him frankly and to tell him all the things she had to say that were locked up in her soul. This is what she said to Abduh the Barber, who rejected the idea at first (as he considered this an interference in what was, after all, his area of expertise). But she begged him, and asked him to please do what would make her feel most comfortable. 'Maybe the Lord would see fit to bring a spot of good luck to the very one who'd never had it.' By that she meant the letter. Abduh, in the end, left her to say what she wished. He was afraid to do otherwise lest these particular words indeed be the salutary ones which would bring her benefit; and if he insisted on having his way, he might deprive her of it. After all, it was Zeenat who was the woman – the poor, helpless thing.

So he wrote down everything that Zeenat had to say to the President: she told her whole story, from how d'you do to farewell, from the very moment of her father's death when she was little until after she was widowed, while still a maiden not yet taken by her groom, who had died in a fire along with the owner of the shop in which he worked. She also told him how she had got on after that, staying with her only brother. But after he had married and been tied down at the neck by a heap of children, she left him, and left behind the quarrels, every day and the next, with the children's mother, and went to live on her own in the shack. And she told him, too, that she had tried to get work more than once, to no avail. Her latest attempt – applying for work as a cleaning woman in the school near her home – had ended in rejection because she didn't know how to read or write. Then, after she had thanked him for the three pounds in many and moving words, and similarly for the eighteen pounds, and after she had implored God's protection for him – from her heart, in appropriate fashion – she said to him: 'Begging pardon, and it's not that I set no store by them, but the three pounds aren't enough to cover anything, because a kilo of meat costs nearly a pound now, and a kilo of lupines has gone up to fifty piastres.' Over and above that, there was the medicine she bought, which the doctor had advised her to keep taking, and it cost a mint. She told him also that she was on her own and was embarrassed to ask help from any creature on earth, whatever the circumstances. Thus she was requesting of him precisely what a sister would ask of her brother, a child of her father, and 'the one in need from the one who is able': to raise her pension just a little, so it would cover the demands of the world.

Then she asked Abduh the Barber to tell the President, in full detail, her story of what had happened on the day of the procession following the Friday prayer service, about the behaviour of the soldiers, who as far as she was concerned were devoid of good upbringing and honour; but Abduh the Barber refused. He refused unequivocally, on this point specifically, because it might result in the letter not reaching the President of the Republic if someone other than he were to open and read it. Abduh proposed adding at the end a few lines of poetry that he still remembered from his primary school days, but Zeenat rejected this, stating that the President would understand the words as they stood, and there was no need to bring the poet into it. So Abduh made do with a prose finale in which he emphasized that the people, all of them, were behind the Hero-Leader in the firm stand he was taking against imperialism and reactionary elements.

Zeenat was very pleased with the letter. She was confident that the President would, without a doubt, respond to her and take the necessary steps concerning

her request, for this was a letter to end all letters, and she
dreamt that the pension would be raised to five pounds.
Indeed, and in light of this possibility, she had drummed
up in her mind's eye the bare bones of a new plan for her
life. Moreover, a somewhat unsettling thought kept
tugging at her. The five pounds, if they really were to
materialize in her hand at the start of each month, were
bound to cause a major shift, a real change in her life.
Perhaps they would even help to make her perennial
dream come true: that dream which never left her, of
marriage and becoming a mother. True, in terms of
realities, there was a lot standing in the way of that
dream, for time was rushing by and she wasn't getting
any younger, and she had passed the age of demand, and
because even when she had been at the age of demand,
after the death of her bridegroom, no sort of creature
had given her a look because she had (more's the pity!)
'no lolly, no looks and nothing at all'. Maybe, though,
the five pounds would stimulate someone to consider
her. If the truth be known, Zeenat's eye was on an
elderly streetsweeper whom she saw from time to time
sweeping the main street by which she sat to sell her
wares. From him she had learnt that many years ago he
had cleared out, leaving his wife and children behind,
and come to Cairo; to this very day they had no idea of
his whereabouts. A few expert glances were enough to
tell her that there was a good chance of extracting a
child from his loins. She thought the five pounds might
tempt him where nature, which had formed the features
of her face and body, had failed.

But as the proverb says, 'The world is deceptive and
illusory, and it never lasts for a soul.' Thus has Zeenat
remarked, over and over, ever since that ill-fated day in
which Abduh the Barber brought her the momentous
news, several days after sending the letter on which they
had collaborated to the President. She had gone to see
him in the shop to ask whether an answer had come from
the President of the Republic, for she was using Abduh's

shop as her address since it was clear and well-known
and the postman couldn't possibly miss it. Presently, the
barber – for whom Zeenat had waited by the shop –
came into sight at the end of the lane, his face pallid, as
yellow as turmeric, slapping himself on the cheeks just
like a woman would do. At the time Zeenat's reaction
was that he must have wet himself, especially when she
saw him lunging for the radio like a madman, turning
the dial as he screamed, 'The man has died, the
President has died, folks! The President has passed
away, people!'

At that moment Zeenat was aware only of her hand
grasping Abduh's collar and a strange anger erupting
from inside her, an overwhelming anger that made her
swear at him, and say to him, 'Shut up! Damn it,
Abduh, shut up! Take those horrid words out of your
mouth . . .'

But the folk of the street, all of them, had gathered
around her, their glances telling the bitter truth which
Zeenat refused to believe; and the tears said the same –
those tears streaming down every face as if someone had
pushed a button to start them flowing. It was enough for
Zeenat to see the dishevelled hair from which the
women's headcoverings had fallen, and the men's
hands, slapping together in grief, to be convinced that
this was no dream. There seemed to be nothing to do but
scream; so she screamed at the top of her voice, and let
out an impressive cry, and then collapsed in a faint.

Zeenat, at the hour of the funeral, did many things. At
the start, she went round the various alleys gathering the
women, to slap their faces in grief and wail. She walked
in their midst until they reached the wide main street,
the route of the funeral procession. There Zeenat saw
many folk and, since with the crowds it looked like the
Day of Judgement, she murmured the appropriate
thing, the 'To God alone is all might and strength'. She
came to realize that the President had been dearly
beloved by many – children, women, young fellows –

and she began to feel even sorrier. She would start
sobbing and whimpering like the children, then switch
back to the wailing and mourning of the women. 'What
a loss, your youth, my beloved . . . Snatched away before
your time, O prince!' 'A thousand mercies be upon you,
beloved of us all, beloved of the whole world.'

Then suddenly she remembered the letter and the
pension. She tried to imagine what would happen to
them now. Tired out by the fast pace of her thinking and
unable to arrive at a reasonable mental picture of it all,
she rushed forward recklessly, leaving the women
behind, and began running in the direction of the bier,
shoved and knocked all the while by shoulders and
hands and heads. She had decided to get a close look at
him, to touch him with her very own hand. The bier got
larger in her eyes, larger and larger, and his features
grew distinct, and she realized that she had got very
close indeed. She flung herself forward amidst the
crowds with great force, pushing this one and that,
giving not a single thought to what might happen to her.
When she got within two steps or less of the bier, hands
began to reach out towards her, slapping her to prevent
her from moving any further. But she surged forward
again and again while they restrained her, holding her
back, over and over. Suddenly she felt the salty taste of
blood on her lips and felt as if she had lost her nose
completely.

Some say that the madness which possessed Zeenat at
that moment was real. But she herself says, whenever she
reviews those moments and her eyes take on a calm, sad
look, that at the time she was remembering how long she
had waited on the day of his procession, after the Friday
prayers, and what had happened to her that day. Thus,
and with no consciousness of what she was doing, she
began to return the kicks and slaps directed her way
with stronger blows, and whenever possible she sank her
teeth into anyone who struck her.

As for the contents of the police report which they

wrote out for her, she said that she had bitten the fat man – the one in the white silk shirt – in the hand because she had had an inkling that he was smiling during the funeral procession. She had looked him full in the face when his walking stick tapped the portrait of the President she was carrying, and she saw him smile as he looked in her direction.

It is said that years after this report had been drawn up at the police station, Zeenat (who had not stopped repeating to herself the phrase 'illusory and deceiving world') was detained for several days in another police station because of her participation in the turmoil which broke out when the government raised the price of bread;* and that at the time she had said, over and over, 'A thousand mercies be upon you, beloved of all the folk,' in addition to many things that need not be mentioned here.

NOTES

Title note: 'Zeenat fi jinazat al-ra'is', published in the author's short-story collection of the same title, privately printed by the author, Cairo 1986, pp. 75–85.

beyond the sun: an expression from the 1960s; when a political prisoner was taken away by the police, to incarceration in an unnamed prison camp, he or she was said to have been taken 'beyond or behind the sun'.

when the government raised the price of bread: In January 1977 riots broke out throughout the country (but particularly in Cairo and Alexandria) after the government announced that the prices of certain subsidized goods would be raised. Many casualties resulted as the army was brought in to stop the protests. Afterwards the government was forced to rescind the price rise; it tried to blame the events on 'oppositional elements' and many arrests ensued.

THE SEA KNOWS

Seham Bayomi

Suddenly, they all became quiet and craned their necks. Although the voice was faint, their trained ears picked it up amidst the roar of the waves, the thunderous collision of breakers, and the sound of the sea breeze, heavy with moisture, passing through the crevices. When the voice came a second time, they all hurried out while the old man remained in the room, still talking.

The girl paused at the door that gave on to the courtyard of the dwelling. She stood there watching them as, supporting each other, they began to climb the wooden ladder; the one carrying the lamp went first. They made their way gently over the fragile roofing, groping for a footing on the joints that marked out the edges of the walls. There, right in front of the house, they saw him. He was standing behind the rolls of straw matting and bundles of reeds, gazing out to sea. They surrounded him and led him off; he offered not the slightest resistance.

He was wearing loose cotton work-trousers, a shirt and a striped cotton waistcoat, and all of his clothes were wet. His dripping hair stuck to his head and brow. They began to hound him with questions; his only response was to shift his dull, exhausted eyes from one face to another, and he said nothing.

'We'll do whatever is necessary,' said one of them peremptorily.

They studied him in the faint light of the lamp trained on his face. He was a young man in his prime. None of them had a clear memory of whether or not they had seen him before on the shore. The girl, meanwhile, was trying to recall where she had seen those features.

'Mus'id, stay with him, and don't let him move,' said the oldest-looking member of the group.

Mus'id led the young man into an inner room and the rest of them left. He resumed the questioning, but the youth merely moved his head without saying a word.

The old man had busied himself making tea on the alcohol burner that was set before him on a little table. He picked up the water bottle, emptied its meagre remaining contents into the teapot, and called out to the girl.

'He looks tired,' said the girl. 'Let him catch his breath.'

'You've got no business worrying about that,' Mus'id said.

Hearing the old man calling, she fidgeted and hesitated, then went over to him.

The roaring waves went on pounding against the shore relentlessly. The water was inundating sections of the stone barrier that ran along the sandy bluff in front of the house, only to glide out again through the narrow interstices between the rocky masses, drawing grains of sand in its wake. The blocks of stone were sinking into the softness of the shore.

'Did the lads fetch more rocks?' asked the old man.

'They've left.'

'All of them?'

'Mus'id's here.'

'If it keeps on like this, the water will reach the house before morning.'

He called out to Mus'id, who appeared in the

doorway, his eyes still on the young stranger who sat hunched over on the floor in the inner room.

'Did they go to fetch more rocks?'

'No.'

'Where did they go, then?'

'They went to sea.'

'They went to sea, to go fishing? Did they go to Narcissus Beach?'

'They took the skiff.'

'None of them said anything to me,' said the old man, his voice low. 'I would have told them.'

The young man stood up. Hurrying over to where he stood, Mus'id began to shake him violently.

'Where have you come from? Who are you? Who is it that sent you?'

The young man's face was flushed; he moved his lips, mumbling, and his voice came out feebly. 'The house . . . the sea . . . the house,' and then he sagged, reeling.

'Leave him alone, Mus'id,' said the girl. 'Leave him alone.'

Mus'id wheeled around to look at her. His gaze shifted back and forth between her and the young man, from her to him, from him to her. 'Do you know him?'

She was silent for a moment. 'No.'

The rapping of tambourines was echoing across the waves out at sea. Fish, picking up the sound, rose to the surface in whole schools. You could see them dancing, their silvery scales glistening in the moonlight. The men were able to catch them with their bare hands.

On summer nights, once the skiffs were moored at the inlet wedged into Narcissus Mountain, the shore-men headed for the mountain slopes. The children, in the company of the women, would have arrived already, grasping their lanterns, so that they would be waiting when the men came. The strangers* would come from afar, drawn by the incense from the braziers and the smell of grilling. Everyone would savour the meals of fresh grilled fish. Then, to the beat of the tambourines, the singing would start. Salama's voice would rise from the middle of the space cleared for dancing, spurring on the men as he moved from one stanza to another, and from one song to another, prompting them to take their turn at singing. Their enthusiasm taking fire, some of the men would go down to the dance floor to outdance each other, holding oars and nets, placating the singing with dancing, and the dancing with dancing, while Salama gave himself up to the activities with abandon, his tall figure at the centre of the dance floor. From every direction the lanterns were aimed his way. He showed no exhaustion even when fatigue had overcome the rest of the group and they had surrendered themselves to the edges of the dance floor, motionless and silent as if they were so many sculptures carved from the rocky ledges of Narcissus Mountain. Salama's voice would still be echoing along the stretch of shore, ringing out clear and bell-like:

Aah, aah, lovers
I beg you, fisherman
Fishing is a fancy
Fish with gentleness . . .

The youth dozed off. His face had become blood-red and heat had infused his whole body. Mus'id, meanwhile, paced around the room, stopping now and then at the window. He stamped and turned round to find the old man's face studying him. The girl, too, gazed at him, gesturing at the youth.

The old man bent down to place his hand on the youth's forehead. His palm grew damp with the sweat that dripped thickly over the stranger's face. His features began to tighten and contract, while his hands flailed outwards and he mumbled deliriously, 'Salama . . . the house . . . the sea . . .'

The old man grew agitated. 'In the name of Allah, the Compassionate and Merciful . . . to Allah is all Power and Might.' A tremor ran through the girl and she grabbed the old man by the shoulder.

'He must have seen him. Didn't I tell you all? It was Salama's voice I heard . . . no one was there . . . out at sea, the waves came up suddenly, and I heard the voice . . . I could almost see him.'

'It's been a long time since Salama went away,' said Mus'id. 'He no longer exists.'

'No,' said the girl. 'Salama did not leave the coast.'

'Salama, where are you?' It was the old man speaking. 'Where are the good old days when you were here?'

The sea cast its alluvium across the shore. Year after year, the shore had extended itself further into the sea. When we came to this place, after a long period of wandering, we put down our few belongings and began to test the firmness of the ground. In the beginning we built our houses of woody stalks and reeds and matting. With time, the sandy shore broadened before us.

When Salama came, a few years after we did, he built his house right on the sea, constructing it of rocks and hardwood. It was roofed with a frame of woody stalks covered in reeds and matting – just like the houses we live in now – and he built a wide veranda shaded by an awning, the edges resting on wooden columns ending in three-pronged supports. He used to collect all different kinds of seashells and line them up interlaced in the sand just at the bottom of the walls, so that if you looked at them, you would think a legendary sea beast was curling itself round the walls, its two ends slinking out all the way to the water.

When Salama sat on the veranda of his house in the evenings, his voice rising in song, the men would hurry over to gather round him. His songs accompanied them when they went fishing on the ocean. He was a son of the sea.

'Salama lived by himself,' said Mus'id. 'And he went away alone. If he had any family, we never saw them.'

'Most of the men came by themselves in the beginning,' remarked the old man.

The roaring of the waves grew louder, followed from time to time by a rumbling noise and the sound of a collision. The spray scattered over the veranda, the tiny, flying beads taking on many colours and shades as they glistened in the lamplight.

'The waters will reach the house,' said the old man. 'This doesn't augur well at all, and the lads haven't come back yet.'

Mus'id's eyes scanned the expanse of ocean. 'We will have to go before the water washes the house away.'

The old man began to howl, his raging loud but unsteady as he paced through the house, rapping the walls and furnishings, stretching out his hand to touch everything in his path.

The youth fell asleep. The girl brought over a wet cloth which she laid on his forehead. When she could feel the heat coming through the cloth, she wetted it again with cold water, squeezed it, and put it back on his brow.

She was studying his features, envisioning the lineaments of the faces she had seen on the coast. The details eluded her, but there was something in the formation of these features that she responded to, that she felt, even if she didn't know exactly what it was. It was something that went all the way back to her earliest memories, here on the beach, all the way back to the first times she had played with the boys and girls here. Back when they used to scoop up the sand to dig out the small seashells and the shellfish, from which they strung necklaces and made dolls, houses and sailboats, as Salama had taught them to do. With these toys they used to delight the visiting strangers on the rises of Narcissus Mountain. It was this feeling that had kept her company all along, even during periods of growth and the changes taking place in her body. She hadn't been unaware of the looks

that pursued her in silence, biding their time for a word
or a glance, but she hadn't stopped playing at the shore,
clambering up the hills or bathing in the sea.

One morning they had awakened to find no trace of
the house and no sign of Salama. On the site where the
house had been, there sat a pool of water, filling a deep
cavity. On its surface floated bits of reed, seaweed and
shells, and ever since Salama's voice had called out to
her, she had begun to wander along the beach. Every
day she would hear new stories about him.

Some said they had seen him sitting on his veranda,
far out at sea, just as the waves had carried him off.
Others said they had seen him running to take refuge in
the rises of Narcissus Mountain. There were those who
had heard his voice singing, and on moonlit nights had
seen him gazing down at them from the rocky summit of
the mountain. Still others were sure that they had
caught sight of him fishing just off the tongue of land that
jutted out into the sea. They said he had come disguised,
wearing the clothes of a stranger; and all of a sudden,
just as they were coming forward to find out who he was,
he had vanished.

Those looks she had drawn disappeared from the faces
she knew so well. She stopped playing with the girls and
boys and gathering seashells and climbing hills and
bathing in the sea. She roamed along the shoreline, and
they made way for her in silence. She would stop, and
call out at the top of her voice, 'Sala-a-a-ma!'

She would see the waters rushing over the shoreline,
devouring stretches of sand and getting very close to the
houses. She would come up against the faces of the
strangers who had begun coming to the beach, and she'd
have to confront their looks, which followed her
wherever she went. Quickening her pace, she would call
out, 'Sala-a-a-ma!'

She used to come toward the house with the other
children; they would all hover somewhere nearby. Then
they'd come nearer, crowding round as he sat on his

veranda, motionless while the waves propelled the water all the way to the veranda, coming so far that it lapped over his feet and then pulled back, grains of sand still clinging to his feet and the bottoms of his trousers. He was silent, gazing outwards, far across the sea, seemingly unaware of their presence.

'Sing for us, *Amm* Salama.'

'Tell us a story.'

He remained silent, and they grew quiet. Their eyes wandered inside the house. On the walls were hung clusters of seashells, and dolls, and skeletons of fish and sea creatures. In front of the house the water had uprooted the clumps of grass that grew quickly there; some of them floated on the surface of the water. They surrounded him again and their voices rose, clamouring.

'Tell us about the sea djinnis!'

'Is it true that they visit you and sing to you?'

'Did you learn how to sing from them?'

'Is it the djinni maidens who plant the white narcissus flowers on the hills?'

The look in his eyes remained friendly, while his features stayed motionless. Wrinkles, wavy folds, had settled on his face and around his neck. His voice came out with a rattle, from remote depths: 'The sea is no longer the sea.'

'The shore has filled up with outsiders,' said the old man. 'They've built houses on the slopes of Narcissus Mountain. No green plants come out of the ground now. The figs and grapes no longer grow. There are no traces any more of the white flowers with their spreading fragrance, the flowers that used to send their sweet smell right along the shore. We used to sniff their fragrance out on the ocean. They didn't know Salama. They didn't hear his singing, and they didn't take up his song themselves.'

The old man stood up, supporting himself against the wall. The girl took the lamp and with her other hand grasped his. They stood before the door.

The foam was engulfing the rocky incline in front of the house, dying down each time the waves receded. The stone masses slipped downwards. At the bottom of the incline the water was washing away the sand, leaving gaping holes between the inundated piles of rocks which were now breaking up and scattering.

The old man started down the incline; just then, a spray of water hit both of them, getting their clothes wet. His feet sank into the water and he stopped momentarily as he felt its extreme coldness. He bent down and began trying to raise one of the rocks. But with the coldness of the water, along with the friction of his fingers rubbing against the roughness of the sand and stone, his fingers lost all ability to move.

The girl set the lantern down on top of the incline and came down to stand beside him. A high wave surged towards them; they clasped each other and hunched against a protrusion in the incline. When the wave receded, they bent down again to raise the stone blocks and rearrange them tightly against each other.

The girl was scooping out the sand at the base of the rocks so that she could get a handhold and raise them with the help of the old man. The exertion was beginning to send some warmth into his hands. From time to time a high wave took them by surprise: straightening up, they would hold each other tightly, and as the wave receded they bent down again. By the time they had finished putting the stone blocks back into a solid row, some bare sandy areas had appeared anew.

'All our efforts will come to nothing if things go on like this until morning,' said the old man. 'We must have more stones.'

The water had penetrated far on to the shore: it now reached all the way to the houses whose owners had fled, leaving them easy prey to the noisy ravaging of the sea. The pounding waves were eating away sections of the houses, and parts of their frames were falling, the thundering reverberations of their collapse swallowed up by the noise of the waves. Up and down the shore scattered pits of light could be seen, moving within the expanse of darkness. All along the strip that bordered the sea the residents had gathered to resist the attack of the waves by anchoring the stone blocks fast along the beach.

She could feel herself growing afraid as she passed in front of those frail, dilapidated houses with their darkened cavities that threw back the echoes of the waves with mysterious, wild noises – those houses that she knew inside out, through which she had wandered, house by house. There, in the distance, on the heights of Narcissus Mountain, broken shafts of light came from the houses that had been built to stay, there, where the strangers lived.

She began to feel her way in the dark, searching for rocks to bring to the old man, to help him so that he could shore up the exposed spaces of sand. Far away, in the waters, they were gesturing towards Salama's house, and in spots nearer by they were pointing to the houses of others, as they chased away the waters stealing towards their homes. From time to time they would be surprised by the departure of some of their number, who left without saying their goodbyes to the residents of the shore. The water would spread from the sites of these houses that could not stand firm against the pounding of the waves for long. Then the people of the shore would dislodge the rocks from those abandoned sites to add them to the narrow strip – once a sandy expanse – below the stone blocks.

The girl sat down, exhausted, on top of the incline. It wasn't long before the old man joined her. He was observing the effects left by the waves pushing against the bluff, most of which was covered with rocks. In the darkness spreading across the sea, little white patches sprang up, all different shapes and at varying distances, soon broadening and lengthening as they came nearer, joining to form a roaring strip extending along the whole length of the coast.

'I heard them talking about leaving,' said the girl, wringing the water from her dress.

'The sea will not swallow its own waves,' said the old man.

As the waves receded, the blurry outlines of the skiff came into sight, bobbing over the surface of the water, until it was moored in front of the house. The youths climbed out. They were carrying some boxes and bundles which they began transferring from the skiff to the house – all but one of them, who stood motionless, watching the shore. The old man looked on inquiringly. The girl got to her feet and followed them. She saw the boxes and bundles piled up just inside the door.

'He hasn't spoken,' said Mus'id. 'I couldn't find out anything at all from him.'

'We've got to act quickly. The car will be here any minute,' said someone else.

The girl's questions were lost, no one paying them the slightest attention as they pushed her forward, their movements inside the house quick and noisy. The youth was still deep in sleep. At that moment came the sound of an approaching motor, and a car stopped in front of the house.

The girl stood up. She stared at the car, walking around it, touching it with her hand, remembering the few times she had seen a car moving along the shore, and the cars that brought the strangers to Narcissus Mountain. She saw the boys carrying the boxes and bundles to the car.

'We have to get rid of him before we go,' said one of them in a whisper. 'He might inform on us.'

'And the old man and the girl?' asked another.

'With them, we'll try,' said the oldest of them.

At that very moment she caught a glimpse of the shining knifeblade glinting in the darkness in the hand of one of the youths. He plunged the knife into the wooden post and drew it out again, sweeping it upward with a flourish. The old man came over, trying to find out what was happening, and when no one showed him the slightest concern his voice rose in a belligerent shout. 'None of you are to move . . it won't happen.'

They brought out the young man, holding him firmly. Just waking up, he was looking around, and looking at the faces surrounding him. When they brought him to a halt and stood a little way from him, a loud scream burst from the girl. She hung on to him, wrapping him in her arms amidst the silent gravity of the group. The steps of the spectre creeping up from behind fell back.

The youth shuddered and his pupils widened. All the while their gazes were fixed steadily on him. He turned towards the sea and made a gesture, and in a quick forward movement he threw himself into the water. They rushed after him but stopped at the incline. Just then the sound of a running motor was heard. As the vehicle began to move they jumped in; he was swimming strongly out to sea, his hands striking the water forcefully as he moved away, far away amongst the waves.

NOTES
Title note: 'Al-Bahr ya'rifu', published in *al-Karmil*, no. 23 (1987), pp. 183–9.

strangers: literally, 'foreigners'; but 'foreigners' can be anyone from outside the immediate community.

THE FEAST

Seham Bayomi

I arrived slightly before the time that had been set and in accordance with the description on the card. Upon arrival I checked to make sure that everything was as it should be. When I noticed the huge gateway, I positioned myself to stand facing it. Some people had already gathered in front of it and I could see that they all held the same card as I.

After me came a lady in a very old black overcoat, her hair coal-black but streaked with strands of white, and then a conspicuously tall man. The way he was shaking seemed out of harmony with his attempts to keep himself standing erect.

An elderly man, twitching nervously, went and sat down beside the wall that was adjacent to the gateway and propped his walking stick against it. We were all studying each other in silence; I was trying to keep one of my feet still inside its shoe, doing my best to hide the front where my toes could be seen all too clearly the minute I made the slightest movement.

We heard a voice coming from inside. The double gates opened with a great racket. On either side, one at each gate panel, stood two men dressed exactly alike who beckoned us to enter.

The two men went through the building's inner
doorway. We hurried after them and found ourselves in
a large hall. The bright lights of the room forced me to
shut my eyes tightly. I opened them slowly; but I had to
close and open them several times more. The two men
disappeared after indicating that we should sit down.
We moved about in confusion and kept bumping into
one another, but finally everyone was settled into a
chair.

Our eyes circled the hall, our passing glances meeting
and breaking off without any verbal exchange at all.
There were individuals in elegant dress standing all over
the room. I smoothed out the creases and folds in my
dress and pulled its hem tightly down over my calves. I
perched on the very edge of my chair and hid the foot in
the broken shoe behind my other foot. The people who
had already been in the hall when we came in did not
shift position at all. It soon dawned on me that they were
actually life-sized statues wearing real clothes.

Those crystal chandeliers . . . the huge gilt candlesticks
. . . Each wall of the room gave off its own distinctive
hue, the colours intermingling in the nooks and corners.
Then there was the calm music, so appropriate to that
particular hall. I sank into the chair, leant my head
against its comfortable, wide back, and shut my eyes.

The sound of a bell pulled me out of my reverie. I
opened my eyes and stood up. A door at the end of the
hall opened, giving on to another large room, a
rectangular chamber with a long table stretching from
one end to the other. We rushed forward towards the
table, needing only the two men's gestures to propel us.
At the head of the table stood one of those statues,
wearing a loose, flowing cloak. The figure's hand rested
on a wooden walking stick.

The smell of food – of all different kinds – stirred up
hunger pangs in my empty insides. Even before I had
settled myself on to one of the cushioned seats around
the table, I was already stuffing my mouth with

whatever my hands could find within reach. Hearing a voice coming from the end of the hall, I realized that the figure standing there was not a statue but rather a real live man.

He addressed 'his brothers'. He said that he was very pleased, and was honoured by their presence; that they should consider themselves at home; that he was taking the opportunity; that this was a beginning; that the time had come; and that he, on this occasion . . . and that they should indeed be happy.

After this he handed his walking stick to one of the two men, rolled up his sleeves, picked up a glass and raised it high, and sat down at his place.

I clutched the knife and fork before me and tried to pick up the food but it fell from my grasp. I tried to steady it with my fingers, gazing at him all the while, but it fell again. I paused for several minutes, not knowing what to do. I dropped the knife and fork to my side and at the very same instant all the forks and spoons and knives flew into the air; all the mouths were crammed full. His features were cheerful and he smiled calmly as if he had not noticed a thing.

I was not aware of how she began. But when I heard the voice I began at once to look around, and I caught sight of her. She was sitting at the far end of the table. Her voice was just barely audible; her head was shaking in time to her movements, for she was tapping the fingers of one hand against the palm of the other, producing a faint rhythm.

The words and tune seemed almost familiar to me; her voice was coming to me like a distant lullaby. I stopped eating. I noticed the man sitting next to me: the regular movement of hand to mouth was slowing down, and finally coming to a complete stop, his eyes upon her. Everyone ceased moving, the food still in their mouths.

The light from the other room was coming in behind her, seeping in amongst the flyaway hairs on her head and giving them the appearance of fiery threads. The harshness of the light broke up as it reached her face, which bore a look of serenity. Her freckles shone, as did a white smudge on her upper lip that looked like a trace of down. Our glances met and we exchanged a whispered word. The man's eyes were trained on our whisper; his features hardened.

Heads began to shake in time to her faint thumping, and everyone's breaths were coming quicker and quicker. A woman with a slight, frail frame was shaking her head so violently to the beat that the scarf on her head slipped down and then fell off completely. Her two long braids, one on either side of her head, began to swing back and forth jerkily. Her head shook more and more as the singer moved from one stanza to the next, changing the rhythm slightly. The tempo had begun to quicken.

The woman let out a strong moan. She pushed at the edge of the table with one hand and her body slipped away from the cushion. She got up, her entire body quivering, and began to move her head energetically from side to side. Her thick plaits swung about, her body reeled, and she began to stamp her feet against the floor as she rotated on the spot. The man's features were growing dark as he stood at his place, clamping the table edge with both hands.

One after another we left our places at the table. We formed a circle around her. The noise of her stamping feet resounded through the room. She let out a sharp scream, clutched at the collar of her dress and, still whirling and leaping, ripped the garment down the front. Her throat and chest were now visible. Her braids came undone; her hair was completely mussed. The dress slipped off her shoulders to reveal dark, sunken lines extending down her body. Her small, flaccid breasts shook, while the woman who was singing moved from one stanza to the next in an ever-quickening rhythm as she continued to sit at her place. Sharp contractions moved in waves across the man's face as he grated his teeth and muttered grimly.

Pressed against each other we stood around the woman. The singer rose and came to join us, continuing to sing. Our bodies were pushing forward slowly as we circled round the woman, who went on screaming, her voice sharp and piercing. Men dressed just like the first two men we had encountered gathered in the room and began to observe us. Then they started to come nearer, and to surround us. When the man raised his fist and brought it down on the table, letting out a shout, they fell upon us.

All I remember is that with a burst of movement I pushed my way out and tripped over the walking stick of the elderly man still at the gate. When I got to my feet I noticed that he was collapsed in a heap in his spot by the wall. I started running with all the strength I could muster.

I came to a stop and tried to catch my breath. I felt a heavy pain in my chest and noticed a sunken line that extended all the way up to my shoulders. And I saw my blood flowing out.

NOTE
Title note: 'Al-Walima', published in the author's short-story collection *al-Khayl wa'l-layl: qisas qasira*, Dar al-Mustaqbal al-'Arabi, Cairo 1985, pp. 125–9.

THE SLEEPING CITY

Mona Ragab

Inflation had sunk its teeth deep into their flesh, and they decided it was time to act. They would have to do something now, before they turned into skeletons weighted down by the soil; and they would act collectively and in a way that showed their anger. They would respond like revolutionaries set afire by the promises that direct action brings.

So they decided. A single shout arose; and they announced their decision in one voice: 'Starting tomorrow, we will eat no meat whatsoever!'

And so they began to eat *foul*.* Following that moment of rebellious fervour, all their meals consisted of *foul*. For broadbeans are cheap and they fill one's insides – and they taste delicious too. Thus was their shout transformed into action.

'We will eat nothing but *foul*!'

And our children will eat *foul*, nothing but *foul*! *Foul* of all kinds! A flood of wild enthusiasm deluged the people of the city – women and men, the old and the young, and those who ruled over them too.

One week passed and the boycott was still strong; in fact, no one had shown the slightest irritation. Nor did anyone stir during the second week, nor in the third or fourth. But in the fifth week a few sporadic symptoms began to show. The accountant sitting before his adding machine said something to his colleague who shared the office. He spoke heavily, dully, his tongue hardly able to form the words. 'These numbers are like the most cryptic symbols or obscure magic charms,' he said. 'It's as if I'm reading some foreign language. Chinese, maybe, or Hindi.'

His colleague, engulfed in a cold gloom, responded to his words. 'For an hour,' he said, 'I've not been strong enough to take care of even this trivial accounting task. But,' he added, 'I've decided to stay at my desk, like this . . . just waiting . . . it's a question of proving I still exist. Maybe, hopefully, I'll be able to solve it in a little while.'

Elsewhere in the city, in a remote corner of a building under construction, the engineer whispered to the contractor. 'Let me have more time – it seems to me that there's not as much concrete as there should be. Some mistake has been made in the proportions of the mixture. But I'll redo my calculations.'

The second month passed, and the city's populace appeared bravely defiant, as if they wore the camel-skin shields that heroes of old donned to protect themselves from the sting of enemy swords.

Not one of them sensed any inner urgings to do otherwise. For they felt at ease with the new situation. Why seek any other answer? For indeed, in the *foul* before them they had discovered the ideal solution.

Their resident thinker said: 'Yet I say to you: we have not given it much thought. We've been too easily satisfied by the ready-made and inexpensive solution before our eyes. We must think about it further.'

'OK, give us your ideas,' they said.

'I will consider it,' he replied. 'But I can't come up with anything right away. There must be another way out, something other than resigning ourselves so easily to eating *foul*.'

From amidst the throngs gathered in the square, a woman let out a scream as she made her way exhausted to the back of the crowd. She was supporting her lower back with her hand. She was pregnant and looked as if she was soon to deliver.

'I feel an awful burning in my stomach. All night long there's a volcano erupting inside of me, it keeps me awake ... But I can't buy any other kind of food, it's out of the question. The doctor told me, "Cut down on the amount of *foul* you eat, and try to drink some milk." But, so that we can survive, we've sold our water-buffalo cow to the people of the city that lies over the river. I don't know what to do ... my belly is screaming night and – owww!'

They suggested to the doctor that he not advise people to deviate from what had been agreed on. Someone said to him, 'Soon our intestines will get completely used to this diet of *foul*, and they'll get stronger. The walls of our stomachs will get stronger, too, and we'll forget that anything but *foul* exists.'

The doctor answered resignedly, 'As long as everyone has agreed on it, I won't counsel anything else.'

By the seventh month the butchers had closed their businesses and replaced them with shops that sold *foul* and *falafel*. The red meat that had been suspended in front of the butchers' shops disappeared completely, and it was as if the inhabitants of the city had never even known of its existence.

The highest official of the city issued a *firman*,* a smile of great pleasure on his face at this wondrous consensus of the people: 'From this day on it is forbidden to slaughter animals for the purpose of eating their flesh. Anyone disobeying these instructions will face the severest penalties.'

Immediately after the order had been issued, high-level government committees met. Large public meetings were held. The newspapers, radio and television spread the news worldwide: 'The inhabitants of a remote, minor city have decided to live entirely on *foul*.' They also broadcast the news that the masses had complied with and implemented the law even before it had been issued.

The news agencies, of East and West, transmitted the astonishing figure: 99.9% of the city's residents were happy eating *foul* and felt themselves to be in a complete state of contentment and accord with the decision.

Not a single case of anger or rebellion had appeared.

In the seventh year, all the shops were converted into government storehouses that sold *foul* to the long queues of people who stood waiting their turn to buy their ration of broadbeans. The private-sector shops sold special, high-quality preparations of *foul*. The city's folk had forgotten that there were things other than *foul* that one could eat and they remained content with the state of their knowledge.

After twenty years had passed, there came to the city a stranger from beyond the river. The elegant clothes he wore intimated his wealth and his eyes held an obvious curiosity. Beside him walked a wife whose features hinted that she was finally at rest after a long and difficult journey. The man was twitching his eyebrows lightly and smiling in the broad daylight.

He talked with them, but they did not understand quickly; he would ask them in the morning and they would answer him in the evening. Their tongues were heavy, their minds unable to focus; they had lost the ability to move quickly or respond with any animation. Indeed, their thinker's fire had nearly died out, and he no longer spoke of alternatives to the solution they'd found. And they could not comprehend the people coming from the city on the opposite bank of the river.

The stranger settled on a piece of land that no one owned and put his cows and sheep there. He went to the marketplace to sell the flesh of one of his cows to the people of the city. But they weren't familiar with this new kind of food; and so they did not even come near.

Only one person from the city got close to the meat hanging up in the market place: a young child who exclaimed with great longing, 'I want to taste what he's selling!'

But the man asked a high price and the little boy had to retrace his steps. He brought some of his savings from home, and with them he bought half a kilo.

He rushed home to his mother and begged her to cook the new food for him. Before the entreaties of her ten-year-old son she gave in. Eating a bit of it with fierce pleasure, he said to her, 'Mama, this is better than *foul*! Why don't you cook some of this for us every day, Mama? I hate *foul*!'

His mother was afraid that the neighbours would inform the authorities that in her house she had some forbidden food. She ordered her little son to lower his voice, or else they would take his father away to spend the rest of his life behind bars.

The man was so delighted he had sold some of his beef secretly to the people of the city that he tried again with another cow. Day after day the boy came to buy from him secretly. The folk of the other metropolis across the river heard the news of that city whose folk were in a permanent state of drowsiness from eating so much *foul*. And then on a moonless night they came with their men and weapons and cows. The residents of the sleeping city opened their eyes to find warehouses full of red meat, carcases suspended high – a sight that was new and strange to them. On the warehouses were hung signs that said: 'For foreigners only.'

The ignorant rulers submitted to their fate. Their attempts to think of ways to comply speedily, and to figure out how they might protect themselves, could not save them.

The newcomers took over the seat of rule and the government offices. They issued a new *firman* requiring the city's populace to work on the farms of their new rulers. They forced some people to till the land and taught others to raise livestock. The people's last remaining energy was drained; their faces bore not the slightest expression of resistance.

The wealth of the newcomers grew. Their agriculture flourished; the contents of their storehouses doubled. They mounted a great public celebration in which they praised the populace's response to their laws, and their continued insistence on eating the *foul* that cost so little.

One day the angry little boy was eating some of the meat, concealed in his tiny room. His mother spotted him and warned him – not for the first time – that someone might see him. But the crying youngster ran from her, refusing to listen to his mother's words. He shut the door to his room in her face.

When she opened the door she was startled by the storm of shouting which greeted her. His whole face – awakened, alert – was contorted into a scream.

'Why did all of you give in and eat *foul*, mother?'

The woman could find nothing to say. She didn't even understand. She made no response to the little boy who was still searching for an answer that would satisfy him.

NOTES

Title note: 'Al-Madina al-na'ima', first published in the Friday cultural section of *al-Ahram* newspaper, 9 December 1988, p. 9. The story will appear in the author's second collection of short stories.

foul: broadbeans, a staple food and a relatively cheap source of vegetable protein eaten throughout Egypt. Though a much-loved national dish, since *foul* is quite heavy it has the reputation of having soporific qualities!

firman: traditionally, an order issued by the sultan or his deputy. Note the use of 'consensus' here too (Arabic *ijma'*) – community consensus is one of the sources of Islamic law.

WHEN THE CHICKENS ESCAPED

Mona Ragab

There was no way to avoid their gathering at this time of day, in this fiery midday heat. Ramadan, the holy month of fasting, had caught them by surprise; it had arrived while they were preparing to take leave of the deceased – still so young – as he began the journey to his final abode. The blazing thirst of this Ramadan day aggravated the agony of their grief, so they agreed to leave right after the noonday call to prayer and to return in time for the evening meal which would break their fast.

A resounding shriek burst from the elderly, broken-down mother when the corpse of her only son emerged from the back room of the house. His wife could not control herself. Pulling off the black kerchief that had been wrapped tightly around her head, she began to rip it apart with her fingernails and between her teeth. The screams of her shattered heart rose in the air only to be lost among successive waves of wailing, for the group of professional mourning women had arrived immediately once the sad news had circulated. Their voices inter-mingled and grew louder, threatening to explode the walls of the house that was cloaked in a black melan-choly. The young widow's tears drenched her face and neck and the front of her black dress. Shrunk into one corner of a large chair, she looked like a frightened mouse.

Seeing the men bearing the corpse across the corridor, she jumped to her feet as if hit by an electric shock; she wanted to touch him before he left her to return no more. But before she could reach him, her legs gave out and she fell to her knees, giving herself up lifelessly to a prolonged swoon. There was nothing the women could do but douse her pale face with iced water: she would have to regain enough control of herself to be able to fulfil her obligation towards the burial of the beloved body.

When the back door to the ancient black hearse was opened, the women pushed their way in, vying for places. All wanted to escort the body of the one who had been so dear: his mother, a female cousin on his father's side, his maternal aunt and her daughter, the neighbourhood women, the other female relatives. . . . Faced with the fierce onset of this surging flood, the stout hearse driver could not object to the extra load. He held his tongue, and in grudging silence he helped the last of them to climb in and take her place next to the driver's seat.

The car crawled along, heading for the family gravesite. It groaned under its burden like an ancient tortoise. Encountering the first pothole, the vehicle leaned so far over that it seemed in danger of toppling sideways. Its smoothworn tyres gave warning of an impending disaster.

Irritated, the driver gestured to the woman sitting on half his seat to give him more room so that he could see the crowded road. With great difficulty he shifted into a better position and begged her not to move her shoulders or hands, so that they would arrive safely and in one piece.

The weeping party was followed by two hired cars carrying the men of the family and close friends of the

deceased. He had been a beloved husband, an affection-
ate son, a friend of rare loyalty: thus agreed all who wept
his passing, stricken by his sudden and unexpected
death. But she – his beloved wife – saw it differently: his
destiny had not granted him the time to be a proper
father to their only son, who had not yet reached the age
of two and did not understand what was happening
around him.

The hot wind of June, slapping her face through the
open window, fanned the flame of her grief. Broken
shrieks began to issue from her. "To whom will you leave
me?" She repeated the phrase over and over, convulsed
like a hen just slaughtered. And it seemed as if she had
woken the women garbed in black from their dozing, for
they followed her lead, weeping and moaning, slapping
their cheeks and screaming.

About to lose his reason, the driver was on the point of
forcing them to get out of the car when they were only
halfway there. 'In this honoured month, offer up prayers
for him instead of screaming and disturbing his soul!' He
was trying his best to maintain a tone of reason and
dignity. His fleshy, red face carried a sullen look; the
veins on his face and neck, bulging under the combined
pressures of a crowded road and the accursed heat of
June, seemed about to explode.

The way was still long when the mother of the
deceased called for calm and silence so that some chosen
verses from the Qur'an could be recited. Hopefully the
recitation would give aid and succour to the mortal
stretched out in their midst. One of the women
moistened her handkerchief from the water thermos and
placed it on the young widow's forehead, attempting to
revive her from a spell of confusion that had come upon
her suddenly. But the widow tossed the kerchief
carelessly out of the window and began to mumble.

'Leave me alone,' she whispered. 'I don't want
anything.'

Since yesterday she had found their presence

unbearable. No longer was she able to endure their continuing repetitions: 'May you live a long life in his stead . . . .' She could bear this familiar and useless – but inescapable – phrase no more. What aid could it possibly give her? Soon the whole crowd would scatter and all would return to home and husband, while she would stay behind to face what remained of her life with a little one still learning to walk and speak.

She was drawn out of her resentful thoughts by the shouts of one of the women, urging the driver to speed up a little. But he seemed to them like a silent brass statue, able neither to hear nor to answer. The feminine voice got louder, pleading with him to hurry, out of sympathy for the ailing and bereaved mother, for she would not have the strength to bear the hardship of the choking heat much longer. His male chivalry roused, he agreed testily to her request – as long as they would give him a moment to allow a huge lorry, moving along just ahead of them with its load of heaped-up yellow cages, to gain some distance. He insisted over and over again that the lorry was blocking his vision completely and that he was still waiting for an opportunity to pass it.

Reaching the new bridge, the ancient black vehicle slowed down as it began to climb. They held their breath, fearing that it would slip backwards. Spotting a large puddle, formed by water from the sewers ahead of him, right in the middle of the bridge, the driver clutched the steering wheel with all his strength. The matron sitting hunched over at his side gave him a scolding for the poor condition of his decrepit car and grabbed the steering wheel with both hands, helping him to turn it so they would avoid the stagnant water. But even together they could not manage it. Just then the giant lorry swerved, colliding with the iron railing of the bridge. Their car spun and hit the rear of the lorry. Dozens of the yellow cages fell off on to the car bonnet, blocking the stocky driver's view.

Getting out to assess the situation, the driver found

some passers-by flocking around the wounded lorry driver. He went nearer to see what condition the man was in, and was relieved to see him moving and breathing. He came back and began removing the cages from the bonnet of his car so they could resume their journey.

Eyes flashing, he froze in surprise. His features betrayed the joy of someone who has come upon a valuable catch.

'Chickens . . . the boxes are full of chickens!'

He left the mourning women with their stricken one and hurried to pick up a cage packed with white chickens. Taking notice, the pedestrians left the other driver lying in his own blood to run after the chickens that had begun to escape from their cages. The terrified chickens fled in all directions – through the legs of the passers-by, and between the gaps, and over the tops of cars. White feathers were scattering everywhere and rising to form a white cloud, its distinctive odour filling the air. Craving that smell, people poured out of the narrow streets and houses and cars. One of the mourners got out of the hearse, for by now they had all recovered – one by one – from their distracted state. She moved forward to take a share of the generous booty for herself.

'We've been suffering from the chicken shortage for weeks,' someone else said. 'It's a priceless opportunity.' The two women were joined by a third, who overtook them wordlessly and was followed by the rest of the women.

The grieving widow shrank into her seat, her emotions overcome by strong disapproval of their behaviour. She hugged the silence of the casket that held the man she had loved. She looked around for the driver and called out, her voice full of frustration. Perhaps he would come back to accompany her – alone – to her destination. But he gave her summons no heed, for he was fully occupied in chasing the running chickens. She remained where she was, forced to wait until he was free of business more important than her call. She searched for the women draped in black who had surrounded her a moment ago, only to discover that all traces of sadness had vanished completely under a mantle of white feathers. A loathing despair crept into her when the movement of the street halted completely, allowing the pushing and shoving crowds to press forward into the momentous festivities.

A frightened hen searching for a refuge away from the reaching hands came toward the car. She turned her back and busied herself with wiping off the sweat on her face. The hen came nearer and nearer, until it was pecking at her foot. She recoiled, hiding in the open back of the car. She poked one foot out bashfully and then drew it back hesitantly and shyly to rest beside the other.

She glanced round once again. No one was paying her the slightest attention. The loud cries of her child, longing for her to return home so that he could be fed, intruded upon her hesitation. She found herself plunging forward heedlessly to catch hold of the fleeing hen.

NOTE
Title note: 'Hinama haraba al-dujaj', published in the author's first short-story collection *La'bat al-aqni'a*, Dar al-Shuruq, Cairo 1985, pp. 5–9.

A HOUSE FOR US

Etidal·Osman

Rami and me, me and Rami* . . . always together, except on Sunday mornings and Christian holidays, which fall at times other than our Lesser and Greater Feasts* and never even coincide with the Prophet's Birthday.

Together, we feel our love for the sea when it is right there at our balcony and when its white birds circle overhead. They come from afar, from Rami's country which lies beyond the sea.

When the sun grows hot we play in the shade of my room. We divide up the coloured crystal marbles: the blue ones, the colour of the sea, are for you; the green ones, green as the plants around us, are mine. Every time, we fight over a lone, lead-toned marble, its greyness a lustrous, silvery gleam. Your little hand always takes that marble first, folding over it tightly, clasping it forcefully. For a moment you gaze at something before you, something I cannot see. You speak to someone other than me, when there is no one but us in the room: 'I know this lead.'

I feel the wings of a white bird fluttering in my heart, and I'm content to let you be the first to take aim. And always . . . always, the marbles run into your row. No

matter what I do, I lose every round. I change the
position from which I will shoot; I come closer or move
further away, or I veer into a corner. I look carefully,
consider everything minutely, and adjust the position of
my hand until it is just right. I incline my body as far as I
possibly can until I am nearly prostrate on the camel-
wool rug;* or else I crouch down on my knees and hold
my breath before the lead-grey marble shoots off from
between my fingers and misses the other marbles. You
win, getting the larger share.

I'm so angry that I practically burst into tears. As I sit
on the floor facing the wall, fuming and waiting, you
come to my side, the marbles cupped in your palms, and
you put them in my lap.

'They're all for you.'

In the late afternoons we open books, lots of them,
bright with pictures. We travel together to the land of
marvels. You read to me, I read to you: about Sindbad
who rode the high seas and came back with a bird in a
cage, its feathers of silver and gold. And about Sitt
el-Husn and el-Shatir Hasan,* the seas between them,
and the haunted house with the thousand windows and
thousand rooms, all of them open but one. And about
the djinni who guards that room and has not slept for a
thousand thousand years.

You are reading. Suddenly you stop and say, 'In
Bethlehem there's a house that belongs to us.'

The words take me by surprise – as if I have forgotten
that you, like the seabirds, come from far away. You go
on, as if to assure me with further words.

'Bethlehem is our city, and it's the city of the Lord's
House, and of grapevine trellises and olive trees.'

I was sitting next to you on the large sofa that is
draped in a heavy cotton weave of tiny, interwined stars
and circles. Between us was a heavy cushion, flattened,
the cushion-cover taut, on which we rested the book. I
found that the patterns in the weaving were becoming
blurred. My head was growing hot and my cheeks

started to burn. I heard a stifled voice, not mine, coming from between my lips: 'God is in the heavens, and everywhere. He doesn't have a house.'

You gazed at me, astonished, seeking to understand. Your almond-shaped eyes, wide in silent distress yet tearless, gave off a brownish flash. It vanished only to return with a stubbornness that pierced my chest. My heart no longer fluttered on a pair of wings.

I was afraid of my own confusion and anger, and of the darkness that now attacked us, and of the stubborn light radiating outwards to submerge itself in the sea. You spoke in a calm but insistent masculine voice years older than yourself.

'Our house was made of white stones. It was built on a small hill and it had a little set of stairs outside, five steps. The last one was split on one edge, the crack would be on my left when I was going down the steps to the narrow flagstone path that led to the beginning of the street . . . to the city of the Lord's House . . . I saw our house turn into a heap of rubble, and my father was underneath it, still holding his Mauser rifle. There were four leads in it, I counted them with him, and there's a fifth one with me . . . in my pocket, it never leaves me . . . here it is, look, just like the leaden marble except it's pointed.'

I didn't look. I remained silent, afraid, my face towards the wall, the cushion between us. I wasn't expecting that Rami would push the cushion away to put something in my lap.

The next moment his mother's voice was calling from beneath the balcony. 'Rami, Rami . . . it's nearly evening . . . come on down now.'

Rami went. And for many days thereafter I felt angry with the balcony and the sea and refused to go near them, and I forgot Rami. I withdrew into a corner of my room, with my many-coloured books and lots of blank, white paper on which I drew a hill and a house made of large stones; a house that had five steps. And the sun was getting ready to begin its journey, taking from the flowers along the house's flagstone path a dark purplish hue that shone on crystal windows, all of them closed but one. From that one open window a single eye gazed out: an eye lit up with brown rays, shining forth, stubborn like the eye of a haunted lighthouse guarding the sea, ever sleepless.

I drew and drew but I didn't know, and I still don't know, how to draw a calm masculine voice, coming from the depths, the voice of a youth who never grew old. And I don't know how to draw the house of the Lord which I will never see. Yet I do draw, often, a house for us.

NOTES

Title note: 'Baytun lana', published in the author's collection *Yunus al-Bahr*, GEBO, Cairo 1987, pp. 49–52.

Rami: a proper name, but also 'thrower', 'marksman'.

Lesser and Greater Feasts: The Lesser Feast, or Lesser Bairam, is the three-day celebration following the end of the month of Ramadan, the month when Muslims fast throughout the daylight hours. The Greater Feast or Bairam takes place during the month of the major pilgrimage to Mecca.

camel-wool rug: reference to a rug made in Upper Egypt of undyed camel-wool; like the sofa covered in cotton weave referred to below, this gives an image of a rural household untouched by new, outside influences in the urban setting.

Sitt el-Husn and el-Shatir Hasan: literally, the Lady of Beauty and Clever Hasan; reference to a folk tale similar to the story of Rapunzel.

THE DAY THE MADNESS STOPPED

Etidal Osman

I shrank in my place. My locks trembled at the touch of
Hamidayn's rough fingers; they closed over me and tore
me from my place on the page with the abrupt force of
one who is angry. A searching look pierced me, passing
through my body like an electric shock from an exposed
wire in the machine which takes up an enormous
amount of space in this place. He brought me close to his
mouth. Suddenly a hurricane carrying a sharp smell of
onions swept over me, reminding me of the odours
which besiege me every morning when the senior
foreman comes by on his rounds, checking the progress
of the work. At the appointed hour he is there, standing
just next to the machine, casting his eyes over it to take in
all the letters and metal printing plates as well as the
final arrangement of the page. I don't recall ever
noticing any look in his eyes but that one dull gaze: a
look that belies the traces of a slumber which has settled
on his body for hours, lulling him without ever giving
him the comfort of sufficient rest. So too with the
morning meal which he tosses into his belly and then
belches into my face. Many minutes must pass before the
dense fumes emitted by that cavity burning with
narcotic garbage – and the clouds of smoke imprisoned

in his bronchial tubes – dissipate. Many moments will
have to go by before the smells of ink and sweat and zinc
plates return to their familiar, diffuse presence.

The smell coming from Hamidayn's mouth collected
in the larger of my cavities. I held my breath in
anticipation of his next movement. The young man
grimaced and snarled and pursed his lips to spit. The
stream of saliva and the accompanying spray showered
my entire body. The froth settled in the two different-
shaped cavities that make up my leaden being and then
the bubbles vanished rapidly. The insult and the
wetness made me recoil even more. Before I could
manage to restore my equilibrium I found my body
chafing against a pallid blue patch between two spots of
grease on Hamidayn's loose work-trousers. The friction
dried my wet body. His frowning features relaxed
slightly at the sight of my silvery-grey colour returning
to its original state, the way I looked before the layers of
ink had accumulated on me. A feeling of optimism and
apprehension combined stole into me, for I knew
(and have known for many years, too many to count)
that the second morning tea-break would be coming
before long.

Finally, the welcome sight of Amm Badawi's shape
appeared in the distance. Hamidayn's fingers, which
had been closed tightly around my breathing, opened
and let go, and the pain I had been feeling subsided a
little. Now I could see Amm Badawi's face in profile; with
time the lines of emaciation had sunk into the depressions
of his streaky Nubian face. He wore the same, fixed
expression as always: that look had never changed since
I first became aware of my existence, here in this
printing press. It was an expression showing neither
interest nor weariness, neither displeasure nor contentment.

The others began to crowd around in the usual way.
Shouts arose here and there, calling out to the
inattentive, gathering the group around the tray with its

chipped edge. On it sat the glasses filled with dark liquid, spoons clanking within as if they were church bells on Sunday. Hamidayn threw me down, the threat clearly communicated in his eyes: his warning to me that the tea-time truce would very quickly be over.

Now I could savour a few rare moments of calm. A feeling of kindly compassion flooded over me. I had the sensation that I stood above the rest of the letters and printing plates lined up to my left and right. My stature now equalled that of the huge machine through whose veins electricity would soon be running, whereupon the madness would start. Thousands of flattened pieces of paper would snap at me, robbing my existence of meaning as I endured the pain. I would try with all my strength to push them away, gathering my forces in an attempt to escape.

They go on biting while I scream and writhe, growing ever stiffer, falling over on my face once, falling out into the margin time after time, jumping to the next line, hanging on to my colleague so that she will rescue me, trying to provoke her out of her passive silence and cringing submission, lunging next to her, tugging at her hand violently whereupon her body stretches and stretches and turns into a straight line.

As to my story with my colleague Ms R* – in fact I really don't dare utter the word quite so off-handedly. What is between us is not love as the word is commonly understood. For the letters encounter each other amiably, intermingling or sitting adjacent to one another, forming words or sentences. The letters follow the course of their everyday life calmly and with meek equanimity. It's a life that seems always to be weighed on a precise balance whose scales tip according to an already-determined calculation. Rarely does the scale tip so far out of balance that talk of change reaches my ears – talk of renovation, revolt or other strange things of this kind. Anyway, these are the things that people differ about for reasons which exceed the limits of my

knowledge to enter realms I don't know. All I do know is
that between me and my colleague Ms R exists something serious, a matter of life or death. Together we can
do a lot. We can perform the miracle of stopping this
madness. It's enough that she extends a hand to me or
agrees to take hold of my outstretched hand. Merely the
first touch will explode everything inside and around us.
We can confirm our existence together, impose our will,
and then the rest of the letters will follow us.

I must have been dreaming. For now here is
Hamidayn standing before me, provoked and tense to
the highest degree, turning and looking around like
someone searching for something he has lost and can't
even remember. No sooner does he back off a step from
where I sit than he comes forward again, staring at me as
if he is seeing me for the first time. His eyes reflect
enormous anxiety and a question is pounding insistently
at his nerves. He can't suppress it, and from between his
lips slip audible murmurings: Why hasn't this ever
happened before? Why today in particular? Or has it
been happening without anyone's knowledge? And if it
did happen one time, or more than once, didn't anyone
notice? And as long as it's so, why doesn't he do it now?
Wouldn't this be transgressing the principles passed
from father to son ever since his great grandfather had
joined the profession? He hadn't done it ever before, and
time was passing, and it was absolutely crucial to resolve
this quickly, absolutely crucial.

Hamidayn had stopped moving. He was facing me,
standing exactly opposite where I was. His pupils had
widened and now looked terrifying; his mumblings rose
above the other voices. I couldn't keep back a tremor
which shook me through and through. But neither fear
nor anything else that Hamidayn might have done at
that moment would have been able to make me change
my stance. The gestures and expressions I'd been
sending out had caused, finally, a convulsion in the
empty space that separated me from my colleague Ms

R. Contact was made; our union took place. Freedom!

I don't know exactly what happened, but I recall a great commotion in which I could distinguish only the screech of the motor, unleashed momentarily, and the voice of Hamidayn, bursting out with exclamations that I could not make out; a great agitation, and other voices, angry ones, mingling with his and reaching as far as the clouds in the sky; the head foreman rushing over, now completely alert, and the circle of youths surrounding Hamidayn, trying to push him away so he'd be nowhere near the machines. Meanwhile, with an iron grip he was holding tight to a steel column as he went on shouting, waving his other hand in the air and pointing to my place. The commotion grew; the confusion increased. The voices were all jumbled together and hands were clasping each other. Solid objects were flying in all directions. It seemed like the walls were bursting apart, or like the world had ended.

Finally the storm subsided. Daylight flooded over me through the thin weaving of the pocket in Hamidayn's trousers. I felt his rough fingers toying with me gently, and on the other side the heat of his thigh was sending warmth into my body. I realized then that I would be in his company for a long, long time.

NOTES

Title note: 'Yawm tawaqaffa al-junun', published in *Ibda'*, vol. 1, no. 9, September 1983, pp. 66–7.

The story is narrated by the Arabic letter ح – a hard H; with the letter ر (R) it forms the Arabic word for 'free'. The letter ح is also the first letter of Hamidayn's name.

JONAH OF THE SEA

Etidal Osman

It was you who took me to the sea, Jonah. You plied the oars, pressing on and on until the shore disappeared and we were alone in your blue world. You did not stop rowing until the parting sea waters revealed a rocky cave open from above.

On the way, you keep up a stream of patter: local gossip, anecdotes. The secrets glide across the planes of your face, a surface broiled by the sea sun; yet the skin stretched taut over your prominent cheekbones shows no trace of those confidences. Nor can any creases expressing wonder at the world's vicissitudes be seen on your broad forehead that glistens with the salty breeze; its oils are spreading outward from the roots of your thick black hair which is shrouded under that cotton, open-crochet Aswani skull-cap. The oil creeps downward as far as the bridge of your nose and then covers the slopes to each side; it's a full nose, without being overly broad, and it gives your handsome face even more beauty in silhouette: a comeliness marred only by that mole on your right cheek. You chatter on, your voice cracked and muffled, fixed on a monotone that never varies.

In silence I listen to you, until we reach the open cave.

You stop talking while you lift the oars slightly, in the rough palm-fibre slipknots which attach them to the skiff's gunwales while yet allowing your experienced hands to move them in that even, rhythmically regular motion. You draw them in slightly – towards your body – until they lie in a horizontal position, resting steady on the edges of the boat. Then you turn to me, your eyes holding a frightening gleam that penetrates all the way to my small, trembling heart like a sharp knifeblade which already knows its destination in the body of its prey.

Only in this moment does your face change. Whirlwinds, whose sources I don't know, blow across it and the mole sunk into your right cheek looks even more recessed than before. Its jutting, uneven edges tremble with a suppressed emotion that, welling up from deep inside of you, comes to the surface in waves which sweep across the skin and the bones beneath, subduing them. I am shivering more and more, my body stricken by those piercing knives that are your frightening eyes. Then the trembling wanes, as my body strains against the far end of the skiff, the end opposite you; and it presses still more, willing itself with every muscle it possesses to split open the sides of the boat and break through into the sea – to disappear, to drown, it doesn't matter. My body feels only the need to free itself from this sensation of terror that is making its insides churn, that is squeezing them and forcing the air out in quick, shallow breaths, as my heart flees somewhere deep inside, some place where the terror cannot follow or catch up.

You did not notice me, Jonah, or realize that it was a lump of terror which sat crouched across from you. You looked in my direction and saw your own demon who had just sprung out of his long-necked bottle. That devilish being inside of you* raised his hand to the mole and touched it, slowly, with a pleasure that engulfed you. You were like someone extracting the sweetness from a sugar lump, sucking at it sparingly so that it will not dissolve before every last grain has released its sweet essence. And when it is finally gone, he is careful to keep his mouth perfectly still, preserving his honeyed saliva that carries the last remaining particles of sweetness.

But the sweetness was not pure, Jonah, for it was shot through with a sharp pain that showed in your fingertips, held tensely on the edges of the mole. It showed too in the way your mouth twisted with a suppressed scream that came out as a faint, wounded moan, as if you were cutting the sugar lump from your own flesh and could not stop scratching at the scab; as if you could not stop savouring the pain.

Frightened I am, Jonah, as I crouch, frozen, in my place. I dread looking at you, and I dread not looking at you; your demon will glance at me furtively and will slay me – your demon, whom pleasure and pain deluged once, so that he told me the story of Fagg en-Nur,* the swaggering Effendi, who descended on our village one day as if he had come from the moon. With him came many books and papers, and giants who moved on wheels, their hearts roaring like the motor of the wheat-mill; and also a coquette who painted her face – but the kohl on her eyelids wasn't like the kohl which the women of the village used. Once in a while she would show herself, and make the ground shake with her every step, with her confident pride,* with every movement of that mass of white flesh restrained into well-defined curves that would turn one's brain.

Jonah, you lost your mind. You had known only wheat-coloured flesh, whenever you succeeded in trapping a woman on one of those coal-black nights. Taking her behind an abandoned boat in the old harbour, you would finish in moments, parting with some of your manliness. Then the woman would slip from your grasp, content with a lemon-coloured kerchief that she would stuff down her chest, the folds at its ends flashing – streaks of blue intertwined with silvery spangles – in the lights of the distant fishing boats.

Afterwards you never recognized any of them, except when a black headveil slipped back in the rush and commotion of the marketplace to reveal a lemon-yellow kerchief, its sparkle capturing your gaze in the fiery noon sunlight. At that moment, your demon would smile cunningly – although you wouldn't let the smile show – and he'd persist in his playfulness: you would approach the woman with a serene and placid face – 'Let me take that for you, *khala*' – and lift her bundles from her.

Never mind if the balls of melting butter run down your clean, cream-coloured *gallabiyya*, always spread so smoothly over your body which is slender as a stalk of bamboo. Never mind if her rooster pecks at you as, its legs tied tightly, it tries to escape your throttling grasp.

Neither the heaviness of the burden nor the length of the errand concern you. Rather, your demon is concentrated entirely in the sidelong glance that you fling at the woman, observing with the full force of his slyness a flash in her eyes or an involuntary movement with which she adjusts the wrapping of her headveil over and around the kerchief, as if the movement itself suffices to chase away troublesome thoughts that have begun to assault her and seem to confuse her gait. Time after time she stumbles and nearly trips; and every time she is on the point of falling, your hand grasps hold of her at the last minute.

'Careful, *khala*.'

You say it in an undertone, the low voice of sympathy or pity, and the woman grows yet more confused. She murmurs things, getting her expressions mixed up, as she wrests herself from your grasp with a forcefulness that knows it has been defeated.

The distance seems endless. To her, it seems a lifetime, an eternity. Time after time, your grip masters her faltering steps. Her ability to resist and pull away from you weakens, and your hand knows how to slip beneath the black *gallabiyya*, creeping below the slit in the side

panel of her bodice. Your fingers sink into the folds of
cloth until they reach living flesh, teasing it gently at
first, then growing more insistent, fiercer, rougher. The
woman chokes on a suppressed scream and she goads her
exhausted, petrified body forward in a movement that
to all appearances is just an ordinary walk. You
maintain a calculated distance, just enough not to stir
up the suspicions of passers-by. Your hand works
relentlessly and the flesh grows hot beneath your fingers,
seething with simmering blood and threatening to
explode.

At long last the two of you reach the approach to her
house, and you set your burden down on the ground.

'I'll walk you to the house, *khala.*'

Her choking voice – betraying her broken breathing,
and shaking with the relieved joy of knowing deliverance
is nigh – can barely be heard. 'No . . . thank you . . . the
house is just over the way.'

But your demon refuses to let things end there. He
prolongs the situation to the very limits of tolerance,
exploiting every remaining second to its fullest. You
pretend to rearrange whatever has shifted in the bundle
and is now sticking out, keeping your gaze on the
woman all the while. Your eyes besiege her attempt to
hold on to the last shreds of her resistance, those final
defences that are followed only by utter collapse or
crazed screaming. You speak again, your face radiant
with the smile of a child who has succeeded in cadging a
few extra pennies from his mother, over and above his
usual spending money.

'Your kerchief is pretty, *khala.*'

The woman's face colours to the shade of dust mixed
with a dull brick-red. Frozen drops collect in the corners
of her eyes while her hand holds fast to her headveil,
tugging at its edge in desperate anxiety. But the more
strongly she pulls at the veil the further back it slips.
With her other hand she lifts it, bringing it forward over
her bowed head. No sooner is it in place than it begins to

slip downwards again. Her tugging motions multiply as her other hand struggles to put the veil back into its proper position. Time and again it slides, back and forth. The veins on her forehead and along the sides of her neck bulge; her gaze swims and she is on the brink of fainting. This is the moment you choose to straighten up and turn around, giving your back to the woman.

'Go in peace, *khala*.'

You don't glance back even once, though your ears pick up the sound of her footsteps rushing forward, as she leaves her bundle to the unknown.

Always and everywhere, Jonah, you emerge, looking light of foot and spirits, moving swiftly, nothing stopping you but a woman wearing a lemon-coloured kerchief with silvery spangles flashing in its folds. No one knows where you get these scarves, each one exactly like the last: your demon is responsible for everything and capable of anything, and you are a child and an old man and a youth who never ages. You repair the planking of boats, adjust and tighten their rudders and pour pitch into their hulls from inside. You paint each boat in bright rainbow colours and decorate it like a bride on the night of her wedding. For long hours at a time you patch and sew its sails. You haul bricks and large tubs of cement mixed with sand and pebbles with which you rebuild dilapidated walls and repair tumbledown fences. You sell the catch in the fish exchange, or – in season – you barter it for a fat, force-fed goose. You are always prompt to help those in need, especially the women on market day. You never change your clean, cream-coloured *gallabiyya* that always sits so smoothly on your bamboo-stalk-slender body. And Jonah, you never grow older.

It was me, Jonah, who obeyed your wishes and went with you to your cave in the sea, where you told me all about the coquette who stole away your reason and captivated the demon inside of you. You spent the long nights at her door; for the coquette is a star in the sky

who lives in the sublime palace and knows how to read
newspapers and write letters – and she will not let down
her long hair for you, Jonah.* Her hair is cut like the
coat of a sheep whose wool has been sheared and is
growing out again. You, Jonah, melt in the breeze
which ruffles her hair so that it becomes like a crown on
her beloved head. And Clever Jonah stands at her door,
stealing a furtive look inside, watching the listless hours
of her life.

Busy with the men, Fagg en-Nur is inattentive to her.
He brings the men together in his dwelling and converses
with them all day long and into the early evening hours.
He speaks of giants whose hearts thunder like the milling
machine: their wheels turn and they compete with the
wind, they go faster than the village headman's stallion.
He talks of iron beasts that have the strength of a
thousand men and of boats the size of the village into
which people settle comfortably even as they are borne
out on to the vast sea. He shows them pictures of djinnis
who look like human beings but perform extraordinary
deeds: they can break through to the seventh heaven,
bore through the earth, plunge into a bottomless sea.
Silently folks listen. Every so often a faint sucking sound
of scepticism issues from their lips, but they take care not
to let it reach the ears of Fagg en-Nur – in deference to
the host, to the venerable stature of the swaggering
Effendi who bestows his food and conversation on them
so generously while showing neither the slightest signs of
boredom nor any intention of ending the conversation.

And through it all the coquette is alone with her
reading, her writing, and stretching out in the breeze
of the late afternoons, heavy with tamarind and orange
blossoms. Your eyes, Jonah, follow her distraction
closely; your eyes tear the garments of her slumber from
a body that has wasted away with the passage of time.
Your fancy romps through folds of flesh unknown to
you, imbibing draughts of a nectar that you have never
tasted. The fingers of your imagination plunge down to

a place that is silken to the touch, you inhale a light which surprises the darkness of your eyes. You go mad, Jonah, as you stand at the door, pinned to the ground, neither advancing nor retreating, your demon churning inside you, announcing his clutching, despairing powerlessness. But he forges on, trying to pierce through to the impossible.

Finally, Jonah, there came a moment to which you held fast in your madness. It was a moment of complete relaxation, between drowsy wakefulness and the sleep of dreams, a moment when all existence lies quiescent in the dusky light of sunset, when the unknown creeps between the feet of night and those of day: that moment when the watchmen change shift.

'Ma'am, why don't you have a child . . . a child to fill the world for you?'

You'd never got your courage up, Jonah, to say anything to her at all. She had become used to your silent presence, to your doing the most trivial chores, to the energetic and wholehearted haste with which you obeyed her slightest summons, after which you returned to your silent existence, as if you were a wall or a piece of the furniture.

For a fleeting second, a sudden, startling magnanimity came over her. 'Such things are in God's hands.' She said it without any show of interest or concern, but your eyes intercepted those storms of buried grief – strong winds stirring in the depths which your words had prodded from their still place; they swept across her face and she was momentarily powerless to control them. She stood against the wind, submitting to the storm – for what harm was there in being herself in her nearly empty chamber? You observed her cautiously, reckoning what the risks of the next step might be. Just as the storm seemed to be subsiding you wounded the stillness with the cadence of your usual, cracked voice.

'Ma'am, they say that if a woman goes out to look at the moon on the night it becomes full . . . and strikes

herself, begging pardon, you know, on her breasts . . .
then she'll get pregnant right away.'

Her head swung around to you sharply, an offended
anger in her eyes, as if she had just discovered you spying
on her nakedness in the moonlit night. Her body
straightened to perch rigidly on the edge of the chair as
she got ready to stand and chase you off or hurl at you
whatever her hand could find. Your demeanour, as you
faced her squarely, reflected the astonishment of a child
who has no sense of having done anything wrong. Her
tension subsided and she returned to her relaxed state.

'That's all just superstition,' she said quickly and
angrily, and with traces of regret in her voice – regret for
having let herself be drawn into the conversation in the
first place.

You took refuge in concealment during the next few
days – observing, anticipating, recording in your mind
every sound she made. Her pallor grew, the reveries
lengthened, and her favourite resting place became the
flat roof of the house in the moonlit evenings. And you,
Jonah, burn; and you can smell the odour of your own
flesh scorching. Not even the sea water can extinguish
the flames inside of you, not even the water of all the
world's seas. Nothing but this nectar which you have not
tasted. You search for every rose which the bees have
swarmed around; you run your fingers over it lustfully,
taking in deep lungsful of its fragrance, so that the petals
shake, unsettled, almost falling off beneath your panting
breaths. You pluck them, petal by petal, and chew them
for long minutes. Your mouth colours as they bleed,
then you swallow them and the voracious flames in your
gut leap higher. You anticipate, and you lie in wait; you
guard carefully against remaining completely hidden
and you are wary of making yourself too visible. And
you burn.

One evening, the moon acquiesced and grew to
fullness and opened its embrace to the coquette. She
revealed the treasure of her nakedness to it and your

head spun, Jonah, in your hiding place: you clutched at a protrusion in the facing wall.

The silvery, milky roundnesses kneaded with pure, clear honey are unleashed; their trembling movements fill your eyes. Your ears hang upon soft, gentle slaps accompanied by the murmuring of imperceptible beings hovering in the sky. A tongue of flame darts out from between the volcanic fissures, going sky high and reaching all the way to the coquette, who is dazed, and no more than half conscious.

You press down upon her with your whole body, you pound her – with your mouth, your limbs, with flesh and bone. In awe you penetrate deep into her, exploring. Streams of honey dissolving into pungent salt fish from the sea rain down on you; you drink but your thirst is not quenched, so you swallow again but still do not feel your thirst satisfied. You dive deeper: perhaps you will reach the honey's well-springs and the seedbeds of the piercing, burning-sweet fragrance which clogs your air passages, that fragrance which has accompanied you, Jonah, ever since, and will go with you to the grave. You did not know nor will you ever know its secret, Jonah. You could not solve its riddle, no matter how deep you went. Even if you had not awoken to the sting of a diabolical pain, the pains of your pleasure were surpassed by what you felt when the coquette's teeth sunk into a strip of flesh in your right cheek.

It was you who took me to the sea, Jonah, and told me about the coquette who ordered your expulsion, quietly and immediately. Tears flowing every time the moon came up did you no good, nor did your supplication to the full moon, nor your unceasing rovings across the sea, living in intimacy with its waves, eating if its fish favoured you, whispering to the coastal sands – grain by grain – about the seed that had grown in the coquette's body until her sleek, taut belly swelled to the size of the moon. Fagg en-Nur, beside himself with delight, feasted the people of the village and showered them with his bounty. He fetched the giants and iron beasts. At first, people avoided them, awestruck. But then they came to accept their presence warily and the bolder ones among them clambered on and learnt to drive them. The old harbour teemed with workers, like swarms of ants, and the fishing boats were abandoned, heaped up on the beach. The money began to flow through people's hands and the women pressed themselves into brightly coloured gowns, letting their hair flow freely; for no longer was it bound up under closely-tied kerchiefs, no longer concealed beneath black headveils.

The coquette, Jonah, saw the promise fulfilled on the night of the full moon. She suckled her newborn on pure honey and the boy grew, a mass of soft flesh that looked as though it had no bones. Sometimes he came out to play with us in the open space near his house.

As soon as we caught sight of him, we would start shouting and cheering – 'Suna's come, boys!'* Clasping hands, we would make a ring, and in the middle Suna would whirl round, half laughing and half crying. We would grow tired of circling round and our hands would slip apart – but our excitement was unabated. A little devil would dash out from us to leap on to the boy, tweaking his chubby cheeks and freeing him only when his screaming grew loud and he ran for home. We would be behind him, shouting all the while, raising a rumpus and vying to see who could catch him and pinch his quivering bottom.

You, Jonah, are squatting there, hiding behind a wall, watching us and scratching the ground with the slender stick in your hand, searching for something you have lost. No one knows of your presence but I, and you call out to me.

'Why are you teasing Suna so, boys? Let him play with you, c'mon now!'

I obey you – for it was you who took me to the sea, Jonah – and Suna plays with us. For your sake, I put up with his irritating, sloppy presence, and I refuse to turn

him away from our team when we play hide and seek. I
tear off with him, his hand in mine, to the pile of straw on
the threshing floor in the enclosure of our house. Panting
hard, he tries to evade me but I pull his slack hand
harder and drag him behind me, not letting go of him
until we have settled ourselves inside the mound of straw
and are hidden from the eyes of the other team.

One time, his hand escaped from mine. I thought it
had been dislocated from his shoulder – but my hand
was empty and he was not there. I hid and waited.

Suddenly, the devils pounced on my very breaths,
and I knew that the boy had given away my hiding
place. I don't know, Jonah, how that blood vessel of
anger burst open inside my head. I found myself coming
out from the pile of chaff, howling: 'Suna isn't Fagg
en-Nur's son, boys . . . he's the son of the moon!'

I was running, shouting. 'Suna isn't Fagg en-Nur's
son, lads! The proof is the red birthmark on his mother's
left breast! Jonah told me so, lads . . Suna is the moon's
son, boys!'

The world went topsy turvy; people gathered round,
while for three whole days and nights – long nights – I
was absent from the goings-on, for I was locked up,
Jonah. I could hear a great deal of noise and turmoil,
and councils being convened and broken up, and the
voice of my father, among many other voices whose
words I could not make out. Whenever the voices grew
faint, I heard my mother wailing in the furthest recesses
of the house. And there were hands snatching at me,
suspending me from my feet like they do the slaughter
animal on feastdays. I scream, and I can't tell that it is
my father's hand pushing food at me from the crack in
the door.

I didn't know what had happened. But one morning I
woke up to discover that Fagg en-Nur and his wife had
disappeared. And you, Jonah, had vanished into thin air.

They said: 'Fagg en-Nur killed Jonah and threw his
corpse into the great sea.'

They said: 'Jonah was carried off by a boat into the Lord's wide world.'

They said: 'Jonah was taken as brother by a djinni, a daughter of the sea. He lives with her now, and by her he has – every time the moon comes out – a maiden whose beauty is unlike anything that the human eye has seen or the human ear has heard.'

They said: 'Jonah saw what we did not: he saw evil coming with Fagg en-Nur, who has turned our world upside down, brought our households to ruin, spoiled our women, and forced the djinnis to work for him. Jonah thwarted the magic. He sacrificed himself for his kinfolk and people, and rescued us from patent evil.'

They said: 'Jonah was swallowed by the whale, like his namesake the prophet. He is in the belly of the whale now, eating and drinking and singing the praises of his saviour. Jonah will return someday, for to everything there is a time.'

And I? I said nothing, Jonah. But I grew up, and I sailed the high seas, and I came to know those godforsaken iron beasts. I plunge into the ravines deep inside their black forests, I sink all the way to the roots of their hair. I sneak into the pores of their skin, I creep through the veins of their metal, I reach their innermost workings, penetrating to their core – and I come back. Every nail in them knows me. The cogwheels with their rusty teeth that grow pliant in my hands know me and the screeching of the iron beast's heart calls out to me when the moon rises, and the call grows louder on the night when the moon grows full.

I began sailing, and sailed still more, out on to the great sea, Jonah. In my heart were the winds of the old harbour and the eyes of a young girl whose head revealed, one day, a lemon-yellow kerchief worn to shreds, its edges no longer glinting. Her cheeks shone like the seeds of a pomegranate still on its branch as she spoke.

'This is the *baraka* of Sidi Jonah; this brings the

blessings of the saint,' she told me. 'It brings good fortune; it brings a fine bridegroom.'

I sail out on to the great sea, and I reach the whale. I cleave its belly, and I bring back its flesh and bones and oil, as a dower for the eyes of the girl, and for the dark-brown cogwheels.

I sail out on to the great sea and cleave the belly of the whale, and I bring back its flesh and bones and oil, on my boat, at midday.

NOTES

Title note: 'Yunus al-Bahr', published in the author's short-story collection *Yunus al-Bahr*, GEBO, Cairo 1987, pp. 85–95.

That devilish being inside of you: The story plays on the belief that everyone has a devil inside that makes them have dangerous ideas or do deeds considered bad. Poets are considered to be inspired by their own 'devil'. But the image here also refers to the djinnis who are imprisoned in long-necked bottles, a recurrent motif in Arabic mythology.

Fagg en-Nur: literally 'the bursting forth of light', a proper name which is a satiric echo of existing given names and obviously carries a sardonic meaning in the context of the story.

with her confident pride: this sentence plays on the expression 'she made the ground shake', i.e. she has great pride, even conceit, about her beauty and walks in a way that shows it; the ground shakes in response. The word translated here and throughout as 'coquette' (*ghandura*) connotes natural beauty and appeal, and moving/behaving in a way that shows it, but not consciously flirting as such.

let down her long hair for you, Jonah: this passage refers to the fantasy tale of Sitt el-Husn (the Lady of Beauty), somewhat akin to the story of Rapunzel in the English tradition. Sitt el-Husn lived in a high tower-like palace whose doors were locked; she let her long hair down so that el-Shatir Hasan (Clever Hasan) could climb up to her. (See also Etidal Osman's story 'A House for Us'.) 'Clever Jonah' (below) combines the images of the folk hero Clever Hasan and that of the Prophet Jonah, who was swallowed by the whale and remained alive.

Suna: nickname for names such as Ihsan, Sana' and sometimes Hasan; it is used for both boys and girls, but probably more often for girls.

SMOKE RING

Ibtihal Salem

They asked me his name.

The letters rang out, letter by letter, across the mouths of guns: those craters of the night. My eyes focused on the rifles slung over the men's backs.

'His name is all that is real,' I said.

In the eyes of the little children, in the eyes of the neighbours' sons, I searched for a child who went out one day and did not come back.

My gaze roamed over the red stains splattered across the houses, circling their rounded shapes, tracing the fingerprints of warm blood mixed with earth. I spoke to the trees and birds. I begged the river to speak, for perhaps the little one had fashioned a cradle from its waters.

I cloaked myself in my unbound hair and wandered about aimlessly, picking up empty bullet shells and counting them, shell by shell. Maybe one of them still held a remnant of his blood.

Still I circled, searching among the people of the city, staring at them hard as I spoke.

'Whoever among you has seen my child, may that person return him to me.'

Tonight . . . the houses of the city ring out their sad

bells and breathe in the smell of smoke. Between one peal and the next, a woman clothes herself in a new blackness. And the siege . . . the siege stands poised at the gates to the city.

Slipping past the careless night and its guards, the moon stole in amongst the smoke rings, emerging from its seclusion in some recess of the city sky. It patted me on the shoulder and passed its palm across my forehead.

The moon asked me the boy's colour.

'Travel back into a time now past,' I said. 'Go back into a time when our city was a place of security and beauty; and stop when you reach the wheat fields. He was their most beautiful ear of grain.'

I began to turn over the children's bodies, burrowing among their backs and bellies. I wiped the black smoke from their faces. I rummaged in the red rings on the walls of the houses. I searched in the eyes of the cannon and machine guns.

They asked me his odour. I said, 'Go to the summit of the hill, where a single gun separates the land of the nation from the siege, and follow the gunpowder. Follow the gunpowder . . .'

NOTE
Title note: 'Da'irat al-dukhan' (1984) appears in the author's recent collection *Al-Nawras*, GEBO, Cairo 1989, pp. 13–15. An earlier version was published in *Al-Thaqafa al-jadida*, no. 9, October 1985, p. 54.

A SMALL WORLD

Ibtihal Salem

'I saw you,' said the old woman. 'The door was shut tightly between you and him and a little girl wept in your arms. A black eye was peering out through a tiny peephole, reaching all the way to where you stood in the corridor, hedged in by the closed door and him.'

My aunt walked the old fortune teller to the front door and gave her what circumstances allowed. Then she spoke. 'She never fails. You can depend on what she says.'

'The closed door, now that we recognize,' I said. 'But where does the child come into it?'

My aunt gave me a confident glance. 'The child? She's the world. Set your mind at rest, and don't worry about a thing. The whole world is on your side.'

She went off to make the tea, while I remained alone, keeping my counsel. 'The meaning of the closed door is obvious,' I said to myself. 'But why the child's crying if the whole world is on my side?'

'I'm going over to mother's now,' I said to my aunt. 'Maybe I'll find the good news I'm longing for, just a bit of good news to satisfy my craving.' I left after promising to visit again soon.

From the threshold of the open door, I stood gazing at

my mother and sister, separated by the *mulukhiyya**
stalks lying on the low, round dining table between
them.

As soon as I had put my foot inside the door my sister
spoke, as she went on stripping *mulukhiyya* leaves from a
stalk. 'Someone rang you at *Amm* Kamel's grocery
shop.'

'Didn't you ask his name?' I inquired, trying to catch
my breath on the sofa just inside the front door to the
flat.

My mother responded heatedly, her voice abrupt.
Sweat was seeping from beneath the kerchief wrapped
round her head and trickling down over her brow.
'There's no one but him who would ring, it must be your
precious husband, may God keep him safe.'*

Silence. 'We were cut off,' said my sister. 'But I wasn't
sure of the voice, I wasn't sure it was him.'

'It had to be him, there's absolutely no doubt about
it,' said my mother promptly. 'And he still has the cheek
to talk to you after what he did? Sure enough, none but
the shameless are left in this world!'

Sluggishly, I got to my feet and went into the
bedroom, its limited space made even more cramped by
the addition of a mattress placed on the floor next to my
mother's ancient brass bed. I changed my clothes,
talking to myself in a low voice. 'The closed door, we
know what that is, but what does the child's crying mean
if the whole world is with me?'

I took my place next to them at the table.

'I'm willing,' he had told me, 'to let you choose one
for me yourself, if that will ease your mind and make you
feel more comfortable.' So he had said after dropping
that bomb on me: he was setting in motion his plan to
marry another woman, after seven years of leanness –
the toil and hardship of my life with him.

'What more can I do? What's left, after the doctors
and the fortune tellers and vows to the saints?' I asked.
'There's nothing more that it's in my power to do.'

They did not breathe even a puff of air into my belly, let alone a sign of life. How, then, can I bring you a son? How, when my womb is not strong enough even to carry orange blossoms?

My mother smacked her lips, expressing her frustration and dismay. Her plump body shook with every movement of her arms and shoulders as she pulled off the *mulukhiyya* leaves. 'When bad luck strikes . . . .'

'There's no need for this sort of talk.' My sister's voice interrupted her, as she stood up suddenly, a fat clove of garlic in her hand.

My mother tossed the *mulukhiyya* stalk on to the table, shouting at my sister. 'You're the last one who should talk! It's been a long time since anyone has knocked on our door asking for *your* hand. What was wrong with what's-his-name? Life is rushing by and before long you'll be an unmarriageable old maid.'

My sister winked at me, and I averted my face from my mother's gaze to keep myself from letting a bitter laugh escape.

'One of these days the man of her dreams will arrive and we'll celebrate, God willing,' I said, trying to lighten my sister's burden. I was gathering the stalks that had been tossed on the floor as they finished stripping off the *mulukhiyya* leaves.

'Mind you don't mix up the purslane stalks with them!'* My mother's voice was loud with warning as she observed the movements of my hands. 'I'll boil them and sprinkle the water across your threshold.'

I swallowed some saliva, its taste bitter, as I went on picking up the stalks.

'Mother,' I said, 'Don't be so sad, it's too late for that. I hear that he has already knocked on the new bride's door, and I will never live with a co-wife - no matter how long I live.'

Then I told her what had happened at my aunt's house, repeating the old fortune teller's words.

'The black eye, that's Dumyana,' my mother

muttered.* 'This is all because of what she has done. She
hates us – just like that, for no reason at all, that old
hump-backed neighbour of ours.'

'The world, big as it is, will seem as small as the eye of
a needle. No house on the face of the earth will be big
enough to hold you, not even your mother's home.' He
had spoken with a certain malicious pleasure, as I
packed my suitcase in preparation for leaving the flat.

'When does my brother Sayyid get back?'

My mother stopped swearing at Dumyana. 'I only see
him once in a while,' she said, her voice taking on a
glimmer of sadness. 'Since he went into the army, he's
got so thin. His face has grown pale and his laughter has
died. What can I say? The Eye, we've been stricken with
it, and . . .'

I left my mother to her mournful wailing, my mind
wandering off to consider the old fortune teller's
prophecy and my aunt's words.

'The closed door, we know what that means. But
why the child's crying, if the whole world is on my
side?'

NOTES
Title note: 'Dunya saghira', published in *Ibda'*, vol. 6,
no. 10, October 1988, pp. 100–1.

mulukhiyya: a type of greens that is made into a thick
soup, a popular and inexpensive food in Egypt.

your precious husband, may God keep him safe: literally 'the
protected, your husband'; *al-mahrus* is an epithet with
which women traditionally refer to young children,
either their own or others. Implying the child's protection, or hoped-for protection, from the evil eye, it also
connotes special worth or dearness. Here, of course, it is
used sarcastically.

Mind you don't mix up the purslane stalks with them!: Purslane
grows as a weed; it is believed that sprinkling the water

in which the plant has been boiled will undo a spell cast against an individual or family.

Dumyana: a Coptic name. Its usage here refers to a folk belief found, according to the author, among some Egyptian Muslim women of traditional and particularly rural backgrounds, and generally of older generations. The belief is that their Coptic neighbours or acquaintances are particularly likely to cast spells on them. This may well be linked to popular belief in the Copts' historical/genealogical connections with the ancient Egyptians.

CITY OF CARDBOARD

Ibtihal Salem

'Be careful crossing the street,' she said to her child, straightening the woollen skullcap on his head. 'And come back before dark.'

She opened the door for her little one. He scampered down the stairs, anxious to get to his grandmother's house. Today was his day off from school and he wanted to join his cousins, especially little Zaynab whom he would monopolize, taking her off to a secluded corner of the house when his grandmother dozed off as she did occasionally.

After the echo of his footsteps had faded she turned towards the bathroom. Rolling up her sleeves, she sat down on the little bathroom stool and opened her legs, a small washbasin between them.

She turned on the lower tap. The water spurted on to the fishes lying in the basin. She grasped hold of one, spread it out on her palm, and plunged the scissors into its belly. She picked up the second fish, and the third, until the water became black and the stink of dead flesh pervaded the room.

As she was just getting ready to leave the bathroom, holding the colander filled with the cleaned fish, she heard a voice calling out for Abu Muhammad. She

headed into the kitchen. She set the colander down on
the marble counter attached to the sink and hurried in
the direction of the calling voice, wiping the backs of her
hands down the sides of her soiled gown.

She twisted the handle on the bedroom window
which overlooked the street as the voice continued to
call out, 'Abu Muhammad, hey Abu Muhammad!'

She peered out, looking in all directions until her eyes
found the source of the voice.

'Yes? Whoever you are, whoever's calling him, Abu
Muhammad isn't here. Who's looking for him, so I can
tell him when he gets back?'

'Tell him: "Arabi waited for you last night at the inlet
till he got fed up."'

He turned away to mount his bicycle. One foot on the
pedal, he twisted back to face her again. 'Please!' he
shouted. 'Please, when he comes back, tell him Arabi
will come by after midnight, bringing the you-know-
what.'

She nodded as he called out a 'goodbye' and shot off
on his bicycle. Her eyes followed him until she could see
him no longer. She went over his features in her mind. It
was the same man who had been before, now and then,
sometimes with two others. One of them – Abu Sayyid,
his name was – owned a Peugeot, which he would pack
to the hilt with goods. Usually he came to the house
carrying cardboard cartons. The night would grow long
with their chatter, a continuous chain of conversation
that went on until daybreak.

'C'mon, Arabi, roll us a few cigs to put our mood to
rights, and then pack the waterpipe. That'll keep us
until I've got the tea ready.'

Arabi would hurry to stack the tobacco-holder,
packing a layer of tobacco and covering it with charcoal.
As the *narghila* began to make its humming sound, he
would pick up a length of cloth, roll it up tightly enough
to fit into a hidden corner of the Peugeot, and prop it
against the wall. Spying the cigarette papers in Abu

Sayyid's hand, Arabi's eyes would begin to sparkle.

'I swear it, Arabi!' Abu Sayyid would say, laughing.
'This is a first-rate piece, it'll put you in a splendid
mood, Abu Muhammad.'

'Even if you found it in the market, captain!' Arabi
would answer.

They burst out laughing. The glasses of tea circulated
with the rising rings of smoke and Abu Muhammad
extracted a few capsules from his jacket pocket. He
distributed them to his companions, reserving two for
himself which he took in one swallow.

The smell of the smoke had seeped under the door,
permeating the room and reaching the bed where she
and her child lay. Her breathing had stopped momentarily as she stared at the indistinct shapes of the
cardboard cartons piled haphazardly in the room.

Remembering the fish which she had left uncovered
on the marble counter, she turned towards the kitchen,
leaving the bedroom window open behind her. She
coated the pieces of fish with flour, set the pan on the
flame, and opened the kitchen window to let the smell of
cooking oil escape. As she finished cleaning the floor,
that same sense of unease began to creep back into her
mind. She turned back to the bedroom window that
gave on to the street; it was directly above the wooden
bedstead, so that she had to climb on the bed in order to
reach the window. She placed her hands on the
windowsill, her eyes sweeping the width and breadth of
the street, waiting for the absent one. Perhaps his
shadow would be visible in the distance.

Small shops – now called boutiques – were scattered
up and down the street, their gaping fronts revealing
appliances, bolts of coloured cloth, tinned goods, various
brands of shampoo, and plastic flowers. Crowds of
people swarmed around the open cartons filled with
goods until bodies and merchandise seemed to merge.

The commotion increased as the prayer-goers came
out of the neighbourhood's only mosque, which over-

looked the streetcorner. The first ones to emerge were some men in expensive-looking clothes, who were practically running to reach their motor cars. They were followed by people whose eyes intimated few resources and whose stooped backs bespoke feebleness and impotence. There were also some youths who had given their beards free rein and wore long, loose *gallabiyyas*, their hems catching in the remains of merchandise, empty tins and plastic bags. Mingled smells of incense and cardboard filled the air.

The four unmarried girls and their mother, who occupied the ground-floor flat in the building directly across the way, were still lined up on their low balcony – for at this moment, after the prayers had ended, the largest possible number of men were gathered. But a teenage girl wearing jeans distracted the men, attracting their stares and approving comments as she succeeded in wading through the press of people.

The balloon-vendor was passing by, as he normally did every Friday, balloons grasped in one hand. Children were rushing towards a small handcart whose aged owner called out his wares – 'Groundnuts, gooseberries, doum fruits' – as he had done for so long, his rounds unaffected by the invasion of shop-window displays. Other children, their faces pockmarked and their clothes outsized, were sliding down a small mountain of sand and pebbles that sat in the middle of a desolate, treeless 'garden' near the end of the street.

The image of her child, absent at his grandmother's, passed across her mind. She'd not been able to dispel her anxiety ever since he and one of his schoolmates had begun going repeatedly to the merchants' quarter – where the largest number of boutiques were to be found – to sell a carton of socks or handkerchiefs.

A few days ago she had gone to ask about him at school. The classroom resounded with the pupils' shouts and noisy horseplay. She asked for Mr Bur'i, the maths teacher. He was not with his class. The caretaker – to whom she had given ten piastres the moment she'd arrived – whispered that Bur'i Effendi regularly slipped out of the school to stand in a boutique of his which he had opened nearby. Sometimes he left a cardboard carton in his classroom and came to pick it up two or three days later.

The caretaker gave a quick glance around before going on, 'And Mr Ali, the Arabic teacher, drives around in his car, using it as a taxi and charging by the head. An hour, say two hours; sometimes he arrives just a few minutes before the final bell goes off.'

Her thoughts turned to the child, imagining him at his grandmother's, playing with Zaynab. She remembered warning him not to cause any disturbance, for Zaynab's mother was still recovering from childbirth and needed her rest.

Umm Zaynab had taken a shortcut, getting married at an early age to a merchant twice as old. He owned more than one car and was highly skilled at smuggling.

When sisterly affection had prompted her to visit Umm Zaynab, she had found herself bumping into the cartons over and over again. There were so many of them! Umm Zaynab's husband brought them home, packed with various goods. Their home lacked nothing, from the video and colour television and wall-to-wall carpets to the electric sweeper, the lamps that reflected their light against the walls, and the plastic flowers dotted about at various points throughout the home, even in the bathroom and kitchen.

When Umm Zaynab went into labour her mother insisted she should not go to the hospital. She would have the baby at home, in her own bed, as the family's daughters had always done.

She had said to her sister, to relax her and stop her screaming, 'Keep yourself together, Fatna! Come on, now . . . is this the first time you've had a baby?'

Then she had moistened her hands in the bowl of hot water mixed with oil and soap to rub the area between her sister's thighs so that the child's passage would be eased. Her sister gave a final harsh scream and the newborn's head appeared, his bare body slipped out and the cord was cut. But when her mother slapped the baby on the back he gave out no sound. She struck him again, and again, and still no voice came.

His hands were dried up and his head was rigid. He was a child of plastic.

The sound of a high laugh that went on and on brought her back from her daydreaming. It had to be Noga Bishla; there was no sound in the neighbourhood to compete with her saucy, brazen laugh. Noga Bishla: so she was called by the visitors of the night, and occasionally by some of the daytime customers who came to see her in the drygoods and cosmetics shop that she ran. Bending from the waist, she would hang out of the window of her home – next door on the right – to laugh at God's creatures as they passed by on the pavement. Sometimes she would toss a few dirty jokes in their path.

Her husband had left her years before, leaving the mark of a razor blade on her left cheek. From that day, her name had been 'Bishla' – 'razor'. These days she was going with a Peugeot driver who was embroiled in a quarrel with his mother and sisters most of the time because he would spend the income from the car – the only one they had – on his own pleasures.

The sun was beginning to slant westward and Abu Muhammad hadn't come home since last night.

She examined the features of all who walked by, the licence plate numbers, the boutiques and empty tins. She swept her eyes into the distance, to the sea whence came the seagulls and the steamship whistles.

The lighthouse overlooked the city from afar, as if to examine its activities and conditions; it towered there proudly despite the passage of years.

Her eyes sailed into a time now gone, when she used to meet Abu Muhammad in secret. They would circle the lighthouse, matching their pace to the passage of its sweeping light, laughing, and dream of a child who would arrive with the eyes of the sea and the stature of a palm tree.

The sun had sunk waist-deep into the sea and Abu Muhammad still had not come. Calmly she drew back from the window to put the light on. She opened the wardrobe and took out a shawl. She put a wrap over her head and adjusted the ends around her neck. She turned towards the door. No sooner had she set foot outside the flat than she stumbled over a large box of rubbish with a big cardboard carton on top. She put herself together and rapped on the neighbours' door. She would leave them the key so they could give it to her son when he returned. And perhaps Abu Muhammad had lost his key.

She went down the stairs, supporting herself on the balustrade. She made her way down the street, oblivious of the remains of discarded cartons and the boutiques clinging to each other. She heard only the fluttering of the gulls plunging out to sea and the scraping of the empty tins against the asphalt.

She walked towards the wall that encircled the harbour. The steamship horns came closer, and closer still.

NOTE
Title note: 'Madinat al-kartun' (1984) appears in the author's recent collection *Al-Nawras*, GEBO, Cairo 1989, pp. 37–46. For this translation, I relied on a manuscript supplied by the author which differs slightly from the printed version. An earlier version was published in *Adab wa-naqd*, no. 23, July 1986, pp. 61–5.

DREAMING OF DISHES

Neamat el-Biheiri

It was the very same dream she had had the night before.
She saw herself eating meat with her husband and only
child. They were sitting at a high round dining-table,
not the squat kind to which she was accustomed but
more like one she had seen on the television screen at the
home of Umm Za'bula, the detective's wife. The
tabletop was crammed with dishes, and she recalled her
mother saying: 'Dreams of meat mean days of misery.'*
She rubbed her eyes, made a motion of spitting into the
neck opening of her gown to dispel her fear and any evil
consequences that her dream might bring, and whispered, 'May God take care of everything.'

When she told the dream to her husband Zanati he
smiled, gave her a gentle slap on the rear and advised
her not to sleep without underclothes on.* With a
tenderness and a playfulness of her own she returned his
slap and then opened the door and left the room, making
her way barefoot on to the expanse of flat roof on which
their one-room home stood.

When Zanati returned from work at midday he told
her that the butcher's son had nominated himself in the
'bedlam', as he put it, of the new elections. To mark the
occasion, he told her, the butcher would most graciously

convey his gratitude to those living in the neighbourhood by offering them boned meat at a reduced price
per kilo, one kilo per customer. She draped her black
rectangular shawl over her head, picked up the child,
and came out of the building at her husband's side, for
she hated the thought of walking behind him.

The dream that she had had, all night long, two
nights in a row, stayed with her. Loosening the shawl
where it was wound around her head and neck, she
repeated to herself in a whisper, 'The meat of the dreams
is real, it doesn't mean days of gloom, it's not a dream I
had because I was hungry, and it's not sleeping without
underwear on, Zanati.'

The butcher occupied three adjacent shops that had
been knocked through into one. Each shop had two
doorways and every door was made up of three panels.
The shops, their doorways and the multiple door panels
were all hidden behind the crowds. She noticed that the
people were tightly jammed together as if it were the
Day of Judgement, the meat dangling overhead for all to
see.

She moved apart from the crowd. Holding her child,
she stood waiting next to the large rock that had
remained in exactly the same position for so long – even
after the many wars that the town had seen, wars in
which she had lost a grandfather, her father, an uncle on
her father's side, and two of her own brothers. Although
the buildings in this street had been razed and rebuilt
many times, the rock had not budged from this spot. She
sat the child down on the rock, patted her hair into place
and readjusted the kerchief that she wore beneath the
faded black shawl. She moistened her lips; and after
glancing round her she gave each cheek a quick pinch.
She peered at her image reflected in the window of the
car that belonged to the butcher's son. He had parked it
next to the large rock, apart from the crowd.

She had hoped that pinching her cheeks would put
some colour into them. She sighed and sucked at her

lips. 'Oh dear!' In her mind's eye she arranged the dishes of food from her dream, gazing all the while at the meat suspended in the air.

'One dish for vegetables,' she told herself. 'I'll buy them from Musa the Cripple. And then one for macaroni – the imported kind, so it won't go all soggy. Another for broth with some pasta in it – the little, grain-shaped pasta, the kind called birds' tongues: O Lord, even though the tongues of the birds in the trees and sky be cut out! And then three plates for the meat – one for the man, to mend his bones, and the second for the child, he's so weak and frail . . . Nothing to suck but my dried-out breasts since the day he arrived. And the third one is mine, so I can go on serving them – caring for the house and the man and the child, working hard enough to move mountains.

'Stewed . . . or boiled, no matter. Or we could boil half of it and mince the rest, pound it and make it into *kufta* with ground rice and vegetables . . . We can have that done at el-Barbari's,* the one married to the butcher's sister, and owner of the mincing machine. Then I'll borrow a lime from Umm Karima, the bathhouse attendant.' She remembered how much she had loved broth with a bit of lime; that day she had tried it at their landlady's she had really enjoyed it, that one time she had gone there to do the woman's laundry. Afterwards, Zanati had forbidden her to do it again.

She could see the moving hands as they stretched upwards, further and further, crisscrossing in front of the butcher's shop. She always recognized her husband's hand, even among a thousand others. It was dark brown, long and very lean and, besides, he had lost three fingers in the War of the Crossing.* She could tell the back of his head from among a thousand, too, for he had only one ear. The other had been lost in an accident he'd had while working as a driver for a tourism company, transporting sightseers between Sinai and el-Arish and other cities. The car had overturned and all its passengers had died, while he had lost only an ear. But he had worn a cloaklike cast of plaster for a whole six months afterwards, spending all of that time in the prison hospital. Regaining consciousness after a long coma (which he had believed was death itself) he had been faced with the accusation that he was a political activist. They said he had intended to kill the tourists, planning the accident after finding out that they were Zionists.

She searched for him among the throngs of people but she couldn't see the hand she knew or the head whose ear had flown off. He might be anywhere, but without a doubt he would come back, bringing with him the kilo of meat. She returned to her dishes, arranging them in her mind with a sense of delighted pride.

'We can spread out an old newspaper on the floor, one that we could borrow from the neighbour, from Amm Hasan Allaam.' She had often seen him climbing the stairs carrying a newspaper and a bundle of cress. 'Now, how to arrange the dishes? Three for the meat, a fourth for the macaroni, and a fifth for the birds'-tongues soup.'

A naïve fear interrupted her musings, pursuing her for a moment: perhaps the birds would come to look for their tongues! But she quickly chased away her fear and resumed her train of thought. She arranged the rest of the dishes she'd seen in the dream, counting them to herself: 'One . . . two, three . . . six.' Then she asked herself whether this would seem a goodly number of dishes: would they look generous enough, spread out on the table? Yes, and as the proverb says, 'Numbers overcome even great courage.'

As for the dishes themselves, she remembered she would have a problem because she had only a very few herself. Almost immediately, though, she thought of her neighbour Atiyyat. Atiyyat's husband was away and these days no one came knocking at her door.

She considered adding some hot pepper to the tomato sauce that she'd make for the macaroni. That would give it quite a different flavour, and a fragrance too. Hot pepper was good not only for macaroni but for all kinds of food – stewed broadbeans, for example, or fresh green broadbeans or broadbean mash. The smell of hot pepper enveloped her nose and she sneezed despite the heat.

She resolved that she would watch out for herself when she went to el-Barbari (the butcher's brother-in-law and owner of the mincing machine). More than once as she had passed the shop she had noticed el-Barbari tossing a penny on the ground and bending over immediately to pick it up. Meanwhile, he would be stealing a quick glance at the legs and thighs of whatever woman was having her meat minced at the time. The woman would be absorbed in watching every detail of the process fearing that as el-Barbari put the meat through the machine he would mix veins and gristle into it and then keep back some of the good meat for himself. She decided to spit in his face if he tried his trick on her. But, she feared, spitting in his face might mean he wouldn't let her have meat minced, on the pretext that the machine was out of order; and so she abandoned the idea. Instead she would just stoop over herself – before he could do so – to pick up the penny. She had asked him once why he didn't get rid of that rusty coin of his. With a glance that seemed to penetrate right through to her breasts, he answered her: this penny was *baraka*, a blessed penny, and it brought him good luck.

Zanati's hand was not among those in front of the butcher's shop. The crowd seemed to be locked in a fight that was drawing in men, women and children. She stared hard at the hands and heads but still could not find Zanati. Suddenly she saw him beside her, cowed and shrunken, like a soldier deserting the battlefield. She thought for a moment. Had his knees gone to jelly now, too? Would he not be able to satisfy his hunger for meat either?

As she gathered the child to her breast she told him that the birds in her stomach, and in the child's too, were fluttering so madly that the noise was filling the street. He said nothing. But the way his skin was stretched taut over his cheekbones told her that something really bad had happened. Grabbing his jacket, she shook him.

'Zanati, say something. Did you lose the money?'

Zanati answered briefly, tossing out his words. 'Half a kilo's enough.' He wheeled around, turning his back on her, and returned to the crowd.

Ever since inflation had got so bad she had thought about finding work. When she had broached the subject with Zanati, though, he had turned her idea down flat, giving as his excuse that he would lose face among the men of their street. And, he said, there was something else to worry about: how would she stop the wagging tongues of the women? They were always gathering in front of the home of Umm Za'bula, wife of the detective who knew everything about everyone's business in the quarter and the neighbouring districts. They would stay there until the evening call to prayer, gossiping mercilessly about a young woman of the neighbourhood, or one of its matrons, who in their opinion had violated the customs of the street – even if her conduct was within the bounds of what was permitted by the Code of God and His Prophet.

Once she had said to her husband, 'The women of our street will talk no matter what. They talk about everyone, respectable or not.'

She set the child down on top of the large rock and chased some of the plates she'd seen in the dream out of her head. No need for the plate of *kufta* – and may God protect us from the wickedness of el-Barbari and his rusty penny. There was no call for the dish of imported macaroni either. 'Oh joy gone before its day, the crow has snatched it and flown away.'* Two plates of meat would be enough, one for the child, to mend his bones, and the second for Zanati. And I can certainly make do with a plate of *fatta*, bread and rice, with the broth from the meat and a bit of tomato sauce, and with some

vinegar and garlic too; the best kind of *fatta*. After all, 'A
clever woman can spin even with a donkey's leg.'

She picked up the child and hugged him close to her
chest. She gazed at the hands hovering in the air,
crowding towards the butcher just like birds hungering
for food. Only a few moments before she had caught
sight of Zanati's hand. 'Where has that man gone? Aah,
Zanati, you've never been able to meet our barest
needs . . . God have mercy on the soul of your mother
who named you after al-Zanati Khalifa!'*

In the distance she saw Zanati returning, his hands
empty. Before he could reach her she said to herself, 'By
the Prophet Muhammad's life, I'll find work; this very
night I'll go and see Umm Za'bula; I'll take her by the
hand and pull her away from the other women and sit
with her to one side. She told me once that her husband
the detective was asking her to find cleaning women who
could work in the foreign school that's opened at the
head of the street. And I won't pay any attention to what
the women say.'

Zanati had come quite near; she could see that his
features looked even more tense and drawn than before.
He was panting, as if he had just had a fight. He flung his
words out so disjointedly that she could not understand
a thing he said. She asked him please to speak clearly.
He told her that a quarter kilo would be enough for her
and the child. Then he turned round and walked off, his
legs nearly buckling beneath him, to disappear once
again into the crowd.

'What is happening to us, Zanati? All this and you
still keep me from working? As the saying goes,
"Embarrassment in men brings nothing but poverty." '

She sat down on the rock, the child to her chest. The
stone was dry and hot, like the butcher's knife flashing
above the heads and hands. She brushed away a fly that
was buzzing around the child's face. The fly flew off and
she watched it alight on a white banner which the
butcher's son had hung up, along with many others. She

tried to read the banners but she could barely make out
the script. She had followed the daily radio programme
'Oh Listener Barred from Learning' diligently; she
could hear it every morning from the radio in the Shisha
Café next door. For she was one of those who had been
barred from learning because of the cotton harvests.
When she had started school in her own village of
Tamayma, her mother had given the Effendi who ran
the school two ears of maize every week in exchange for
her schooling. But then her mother had taken her out of
school during the cotton harvest so that she could bring
her mother five- and ten-piastre pieces.

She had gone on listening hungrily to the radio
programme for two whole years, longing to read. And
indeed she had begun reading signs on shops and in the
covered market areas, but she did not understand
anything. She would hear of 'The Honesty Grocery' and
'The Fidelity Sweetshop', of 'Freedom Snacks' and
'The Victory Wheelmaker', and she understood the
meaning of these names, every one, but she could not
match them to the shop signs, so she tried to make out
the letters. But the very same names faded away like the
smoke from Zanati's waterpipe. Instead, she began to
read 'Chipsy' and 'Seven Up' and 'Dolce', and to keep
track of the formidable number of billboard ads which
towered over the pavements and topped the façades of
shops and stores.

The election banners were all over the street. She
remembered going a few days before to buy some calico
– just the plain white kind – to have underclothes for
Zanati and pillowcases made up, but she hadn't been
able to find any. With difficulty she read the banner,
which was made of the same white calico: 'Elect *ibn
el-dayra*, the son of this precinct', followed by the name of
the butcher's son. Uneasily, she repeated the phrase to
herself. '*Ibn el-dayra*,* son of.... Just like that, out in the
open, the brazen fellow! Times have changed, Zanati,
and you still scold me for wanting to work.'

She picked up the child, gazing at the banners and wishing she could come here after nightfall, climb on top of the rock and rip down this banner, and that one, and the third one too, without being seen by anyone. Then she would go home and soak them in water for the rest of the night. In the morning she would take the banners to the seamstress, who would make pillowcases and under-clothes for Zanati out of them. As for 'the son of the precinct', well, he would win whether he had the banners or not.

The second plate of meat faded from her mind. The little birds came and retrieved their tongues. Only one plate of meat to dream of now. She glanced at the banners and then at the men crowded in front of the butcher's shop. Maybe all those men lacked under-clothes, just like Zanati.

'I'll boil the quarter kilo and put it in a large bowl with half the broth, and the rest of the juice I'll use to make a dish of *fatta* and rice in tomato sauce with vinegar and garlic. A quarter kilo will barely take the edge off his hunger, and the child's too.' As for herself, she would go that night to the detective's wife and ask her to arrange a job at the school.

But her mind came back to the old problem. What would she do about Zanati? Would he accept her plan? She resolved to stand up to him this time, if he didn't approve, or answer her nicely. After all, why had he agreed to the idea of her leaving the country to work? He hadn't seemed to mind when she had brought up the subject; she had told him that she could work as a nursemaid – just like Gaber's wife was doing – in one of the Gulf States. But at the time she had had second thoughts – 'Being far from home is hateful, Zanati,' she had said – and had dropped the idea.

Now she began to ask herself: 'How could he decide it was all right for me to travel abroad, but not for me to work practically next door, so close to the flat and the child?' She wondered whether he loved her. She

remembered the day he had told her that just this once
he was thinking about going away, in search of work.
She had sworn to him by the God-given bread they ate
that even if she had nothing but salt to dip it in, he would
not sleep a single night away from her.

Zanati was coming back, empty handed, his face
showing defeat. She said nothing; she asked him nothing.
She picked up the child, stood up from the sharp rock
and chased the last of the dream dishes out of her head.
She threw a last glance at the banners of the nominee,
'son of the precinct', and then at the men in the crowd.

A fold of her *gallabiyya* clung in between her buttocks.
She yanked the gown loose and began walking beside
her husband. Her legs felt full of pins and needles, as if
they had gone to sleep, or as if they were crawling with
ants. She imagined swarms of ants gathering round her
head, and then they began to creep down all over her.

NOTES

Title note: 'Atbaq fi'l-hulm' appears in the author's
second collection of short stories, *Al-'Ashiqun* (*The
Lovers*), GEBO, Cairo 1989. The story, translated from a
manuscript provided by the author, was written in May
1987.

'*Dreams of meat mean days of misery*': more literally, 'Meat
in a dream is a sad and depressing thing'; this bespeaks
the folk belief that the opposite of what appears in your
dream is likely to happen.

not to sleep without underclothes on: literally, 'not to sleep
naked', but meaning idiomatically without underclothes,
or having one's nightclothes slip up around one's body
while sleeping. The expression is said to or of someone
who has had a bad dream.

El-Barbari: here, a proper name, but the term has
derisive connotations, suggesting someone 'primitive' or
'bad-tempered'.

War of the Crossing: a reference to the October 1973 War, when Egyptian troops crossed the Suez Canal into the Sinai, occupied at the time by Israel.

O joy gone . . .: A proverb said when an individual obtains something which brings happiness, only to find it soon lost and gone. The crow is an image of misfortune, and is seen as a bringer of bad news, an omen of unhappiness or impending tragedy.

Al-Zanati Khalifa: the major villain in a famous folk epic, *The Hilaliyya*, versions of which are still sung and recited throughout much of the Arab world and in parts of sub-Saharan Africa, often injected with local nationalist symbols and messages. The Khalifa Zanati is the Berber ruler of Tunis; he was defeated by Abu Zayd al-Hilali and his fellow tribesmen who had migrated westward from the Arabian peninsula.

dayra: here, as a defined administrative or electoral district, but according to the author the character is recalling another, slang meaning, as 'a woman who circulates', i.e. a streetwalker.

YOUR FACE, MY CHILDREN
AND THE OLIVE BRANCHES

Neamat el-Biheiri

As day after day came and went, there was nothing to relieve the relentless ennui which seemed to split me in two. At home the face of a severe and miserly father stalked me, trying to force my liberation from the papers and history books cluttering my room and holding me captive. According to his way of thinking, they wouldn't provide us with even the nourishment of bread eaten dry, on its own. His voice would surround and beleaguer me until I would fly in panicky fright from the cold walls enveloping me, and from his advice. It would be more useful to both of us, he claimed, for me to learn a European language.

At school the faces of my small pupils gazed at me. In their brightly coloured clothes, wearing hairbands over their long, flowing hair, they studied me shyly out of frightened eyes. They listened silently as I spilled history lessons into their ears, while the commotion coming from the street put a barrier between us.

In spite of the noise I began to tell them proudly about my grandmother Isis. My students' eyes took on a sparkle. We were all captivated, our state of alertness lasting until the sound of the bell reached our ears. The rows of students broke up to leave the room, myself among them.

In the street only my briefcase and history books accompanied me. Like someone under hypnosis I wandered among the pedestrians, their shoulders knocking against me. I raised my head to look at the old buildings lining the streets of downtown Cairo. This was the first time, I recalled, that I had noticed the façades on both sides of the street reflecting the styles characteristic of old European architecture: the defeated face of Napoleon and the slain countenance of Kleber* gazed down upon me. Despite the heaviness of my gait I felt that the defeated and slain faces were driving me towards the river – that same river into which, my mother once told me, she had thrown my afterbirth on the day I was born.* I loved the river with the same passion that marked my tireless search for deliverance.

The face of my grandmother Isis accompanied me as I made my way to the river – Isis, ever searching for the shreds of the lover who has not yet gone away.

At the river all the voices and sounds disappeared, leaving only your voice, filled with entreaty. I searched for the voice's owner and saw a shape that resembled your face. It was settling on to an approaching wave, a billow still in the distance.

Alone, the head floated over the river's surface. I searched in the folds of that face and saw you. The flowers on the riverbank cheered, rejoicing along with me.

I apologize, my friend and mentor: today, like a tree shorn of its leaves, I have been stripped bare of paper.

But when I saw your face (when the sun suddenly broke forth, having given no prior hint of appearing, for a wave of cold had raged since morning), I hurried over to one of the figures seated, like me, in solitude. I begged him to blot out my nakedness with a leaf of paper, a scrap on which I could address you.

In a single moment the sun rises and sets dozens of

times, and the newly built edifices surround and enclose
me. Tears that my mother used to call 'tears of joy' jump
to my eyes. Your dark face and your eyes draw near, the
colour of your pupils – now visible – mingling with the
blueness of our vast river. I begin to feel hatred for all
men on earth except you. I seek your face across
distances strewn with the tears of the men who lament
me, mourning a free and upright woman from the land
of slaves and concubines.

I drew nearer to the riverbank. As I pressed my body
against it my spirits, churned up since yesterday night's
slow passage, regained their tranquillity. I cleansed my
face seven times in the water of the wave bearing your
head to me. Then I drank from the same water, filled my
palms and baptized my body.

I sensed the tremor that had lived inside of me for a
long time beginning to subside, and then it faded away.
The wind slapped my face, bringing the fresh water
seeping into my pores, to leave a sensation of sweetness. I
felt deliriously happy. There were many, many children
crowding inside my body, jostling each other for space,
and I had no choice but to give birth to them. I drew
away slightly from the river and stretched out on the
green. I could see the children slipping out painlessly to
scamper about in delight, the sun blessing their faces,
and tossing their afterbirths into the great river. Each
and every one of them ran immediately to the river and
took their places atop the wave just next to yours. Each
child held an olive branch in one hand and with the
other grasped a white dove. They circled round your
face, laughing and shouting. I wasn't familiar with the
language they spoke, but you were laughing. That lock
of hair, now tinged with grey, was playing on your
forehead. I couldn't believe what was happening around
me. For a long moment I seemed to be in a state of
numbness. Your eyes were kissing me, sending me into
ecstasy. I joined in our children's playing, in their
cheering and shouting.

The circle expands. Around you flutter the olive branches, the white doves and the ancient Egyptian songs.

Our children had the sweetness of the sun, and its warmth too. Their eyes bore the blueness of the mighty river. Their bodies had the towering height of the date-palms, the stature of our other trees. Their hair was as thick as the green orchard grass growing on the very edges of the riverbanks. I saw the waves making you bob and dance, you and them. The children's voices rose, singing in harmony with the river. The others, far away from us, were attracted by our own, private joy. They cheered and clapped for our children, and a feeling of happiness came over all of us. I began thanking the Lord reflected in their eyes.

Suddenly and unexpectedly the wave split to reveal the head of a voracious crocodile, ploughing through the billowing waters of the river, distancing me from the ring over which fluttered the olive branches. I screamed as he drew you, along with them, far away from the riverbank. I tried to throw myself in, to follow you, but the huge throngs of people came between us and impeded me. The crocodile split the circle in two and began to devour one figure after another.

The crocodile was huge and multicoloured – red and blue and some white. His sharp jaws extended further than I could see. My children had disappeared completely: between the crocodile's jaws could be seen only the olive branches and the white doves, which he went on eating greedily. Your eyes overflowed with tears, and then you were hidden behind the waves.

I folded up my scraps of paper and walked along, following the path of the mighty river. I could see blood covering its surface. The remnants of the olive branches were also bloodstained, while the white dove feathers flocked together, to sink and float over the redness of the waters. I turned my back on the river and walked on. I was trying hard to find a way to excuse the great river for its predatory crocodiles.

NOTES

Title note: 'Wajhuka, atfali, wa aghsan al-zaytun', published in *Ibda'*, vol. 3, no. 12, December, 1985, pp. 89–90.

Kleber: one of the generals who accompanied Napoleon Bonaparte on his expedition to Egypt in 1798. After Napoleon's departure, Kleber succeeded him as commander of the French troops in Egypt, from August 1799 to June 14 1800, when he was assassinated by a local resident.

my afterbirth: reference to a custom with ancient Egyptian roots; throwing the afterbirth into the Nile is most likely linked to the legends surrounding the gods Isis and Osiris. It is considered to be a sort of offering to the Nile as the giver of life, an act of recognition of the ongoing life process. The word *khalaas*, used in the next sentence, expresses this, for it means both 'deliverance' or 'salvation' and 'placenta'.

THE WAY TO THE SEVENTH

Neamat el-Biheiri

When the disc of the sun fragments, when it turns into golden shreds that dissolve into nothingness behind the tall trees rising between the Sixth Quarter and the Seventh,* a limpid daylight spreads across the sky and eight-year-old Ula knows that Umm al-Ghanam* is coming. Ula brushes the dirt from her small palms, dusts off her short dress, and runs towards the trees, chanting out her call repeatedly like a pretty song.

'Umm al-Ghanam! Umm al-Ghanam! Umm al-Ghanam is coming!'

Ula had given her this name, for the little girl had known no other name for her since becoming aware of the world around her and learning to distinguish among faces and things.

Appearing in the distance, the woman looks like a black speck, moving amongst a flock of sheep under the guard of a skinny black dog. The black speck moves again and its shadow is lost amidst the sheep. Drawing nearer, it takes shape and turns into the lines of a woman concealed in a black gypsy gown. No one here has seen her face or heard her voice. She leaves her sheep with the dog to graze on the *gabal*, that dirt-surfaced open plateau which stretches before the blocks of council flats.

She seats herself on a gentle and welcoming rock,
stretching her legs out over the dirt, no part of her visible
but the silver anklets that rest just above her henna-dyed
feet.

Before Umm al-Ghanam arrives Ula has used up half
of her day, playing in the dirt with the children from the
blocks of flats while the women call out to her. 'Ula, go
there . . . Ula, come here . . . Take this, and bring me
that, Ula!' One of the women gives her food left over
from the day before that her own children have rejected
angrily. Another asks her to buy something. A neighbour
opens her window, sucking her lips and querying, 'Ula,
Ula . . . If names had to be bought with money . . . .'* She
swallows the other half of the proverb along with
whatever is in her mouth as she gazes at Ula's father in
his striped *gallabiyya*, sitting hunched over on his ancient
wooden stool in the sun. In his hearing she repeats her
words – 'Ula, Ula . . . If names had to be bought with
money . . .' – and her faint laughs rise in rapid
succession. Her words and glances, and even the
tenderness she showers on his daughter from time to
time, carry more than a little flirtatiousness towards
Ula's father. The child finds her show of affection
distasteful and goes on observing Umm al-Ghanam's
approach as she comes towards them from the Seventh
Quarter.

Umm al-Ghanam's eyes were following the movements of her sheep and the skinny dog that served as
their guard. Every day she would leave them to graze in
the dirt of the *gabal* fronting the blocks of flats, for
without a doubt they would find their day's nourishment
here: a dead chicken or a sheep's head already gnawed
to the bone; the corpse of a newborn whose adulterous
mother, after strangling her baby, has gone away with
the night; or the remnants left over from cleaning the
chicken legs which the residents of the blocks buy by the
kilo.

Umm al-Ghanam was scratching at the dirt with her

stick when she spotted two dirty little feet covered with the marks of dried-out wounds. This was the first time that Ula had come close to Umm al-Ghanam, her reticence overcome by a longing to see the woman's face. Umm al-Ghanam's eyes were a strange colour, their spherical, shining blackness sharply outlined in the intensity of the surrounding whiteness. Umm al-Ghanam was not like the women who lived in the blocks of flats. She was calm and silent while those women all fawned on her father, making up to her, even that woman – their neighbour – who really would have liked Ula to call her 'mother' but then thought better of it.

Ula gazed towards the tall trees at the end of the blocks. The sight of the sun dissolving behind the towering buildings of the Seventh gave her a sense of comfort and pleasure. For a long time now she had wanted to speak to Umm al-Ghanam, even if only once. To be exact, she had felt this yearning ever since her mother had gone to the Seventh and hadn't come back. And then ever since the woman her father had married had gone there never to return, and her uncle too . . .

'Have you seen any of them in the Seventh?' Ula asked Umm al-Ghanam.

The woman did not answer. She appeared to have heard nothing of what Ula had said. Ula thought about telling Umm al-Ghanam what she had once told her mother, whereupon her mother had beaten her. And what she had told her uncle's wife, who then had scolded her, and what she had told her father's wife, whereupon her father had beaten her, and what she had told her father's dog, who had bitten her.

'Have you been through the Seventh?' Ula asked Umm al-Ghanam.

It seemed that the woman had heard nothing this time either. She had begun to pull down her black *niqab** with its trim of gold and silvery spangles. This was the first time that Ula had seen Umm al-Ghanam's face. She was amazed by those thinly-etched blue lines that descended vertically from just below Umm al-Ghanam's lower lip to the tip of her chin, and that gold ring dangling from her nose, and the coal-black hair to which henna had given a reddish-orange tint.

'The children from the blocks say the Seventh is a whole different world,' said Ula to Umm al-Ghanam.

The woman laughed and, her voice faint, mumbled something which the girl did not understand. Ula thought about telling Umm al-Ghanam what she had once told the mudbricks scattered in front of the blocks of flats. She remembered that Umm al-Ghanam never responded when the children from the blocks of flats teased her. When the men flung flirtatious comments at her, she paid them no attention. And whenever the women drew near to ask about the Seventh Quarter and the women and men who lived there, she would slip away from them. For just as Umm al-Ghanam came in silence, she left in silence too.

So Ula began telling Umm al-Ghanam about her day: that she goes out in the morning after bringing her father his breakfast and cigarettes, and sits down on the corner of the main street next to the station-inspector's booth. She watches the private cars that go up the slope of ground dividing the Sixth and the Seventh, moving very slowly, while others descend at high speed as if they are sliding down a mountain. In the car windows she sees dogs that are clean and handsome and bear no resemblance to her father's dog or the dogs that one sees in the blocks of flats.

Umm al-Ghanam said nothing. But Ula started telling her anyway that she hated the blocks, for they were stifling and cramped and filthy, and she hated the people who lived in them too. She hated her father and mother, her father's wife and her uncle's wife, and also her father's dog and the mudbricks on the *gabal* and the soldiers from the military camps. Those camps were separated from the blocks only by barbed wire. Many times she had ripped her dress when crossing the barbed

wire with the children from the council blocks to pick
the small black grapes on their squat, thickly growing
bushes. The children called them 'wolves' grapes'.

Once she asked a soldier – whose face was as black as
the grapes, so she thought he was a 'wolves' soldier' –
'Do you know the way to the Seventh?'

When he nodded, she shook the dust from her dress
and said to him, 'Take me there.'

That day, the dusky soldier had grasped her hand and
pulled her along until they had passed the tall trees
rising between the two quarters. He hid with her amidst
the wolves' grapes bushes with their sharp thorns and
began to kiss her and suck at her lips and cover her face
and body with his saliva. That day, Ula bit him just as if
she were her father's dog and ran off, leaving her dress
for him. She began cursing to herself, cursing the
Seventh and the images of it which the women and
children from the blocks had stirred up in her mind.

As Ula told Umm al-Ghanam her story, her little face
went white. The woman patted her on the shoulder and
kissed her. From her dust-covered black knapsack she
drew out an ivory comb and a bit of broken mirror the
size of her palm. She began to comb Ula's hair.

Ula always tied her hair back into a ponytail, for her
father would shout at her if she left it to swing freely in
the air, just as her mother used to scold her if she saw it
unbound and falling down Ula's back. And whenever
her uncle's wife had seen Ula combing it she had chided
the girl. In the piece of broken mirror Ula saw her hair,
long and flowing, draping itself over her shoulders like a
silken shawl of the same hue as her honey-coloured eyes.
Ula looked just like a pretty butterfly, dipping through
the air.

Ula smiled, revealing her broken tooth. The woman
beckoned to her sheep and dog with the stick in her
hand, preparing to leave.

Ula tugged at the woman's shoulder. 'When you
come tomorrow,' Ula said, 'I'll tell you other things,

because I haven't told you everything yet.'

NOTES
Title note: Written in January 1988. First published as
'Umm al-Ghanam' in *Ibda'*, vol. 6, no. 5, May 1988, pp.
111–12. A revised version, translated here, is published
as 'Al-Tariq ila al-Sabi' ' in el-Biheiri's second collection, *al-'Ashiqun*, GEBO, Cairo 1989.

Sixth and Seventh Quarters: Two large, adjacent neigh-
bourhoods in Madinat Nasr (Victory City), an urban
extension of Cairo stretching north-west into the desert.
The Sixth Quarter was populated after the 1967 War by
families fleeing cities that had been bombed. They were
housed in government-built blocks of flats. Following
their return to their home cities, the flats were given to
residents of older areas of Cairo whose buildings had
collapsed. Whole resident groups moved *en masse*,
preserving the original composition and arrangement of
their neighbourly relations in the new locations. The
government is now allowing residents to purchase their
flats in monthly instalments. The dreary buildings are
densely populated and in bad repair.

The Seventh Quarter is made up of privately
constructed flats owned or rented by higher-income
families, many of whom emigrated to work in the Gulf
countries or elsewhere and upon their return purchased
real estate. Others made their money through commercial projects begun under Sadat's Open-Door Policy
of the early 1970s. Many women from the Sixth Quarter
work as domestics in the Seventh.

Umm al-Ghanam: literally 'mother of the sheep'; traditional nomenclature by which a mother is called by the
name of her eldest child or eldest son. By extension, this
usage becomes a possessive: i.e., 'she who has sheep'.

'*If names were bought with money* . . .': The rest of the
proverb, which is usually left unsaid, is translated as: '. . .

then the poor person would name his son Shit.' The nearest English eqivalent is 'What's in a name?' 'Ula' means 'high rank' or 'nobility'.

niqab: here, the traditional face-veil (*burqa'*) which covers the lower part of the face and is stretched over the nose so that only the eyes appear. It is usually made of black crêpe or silk and decorated with sequins or spangles of gold, silver or copper, depending on the wearer's economic standing. It is still worn in Egypt by Bedouin women and is not to be confused with the *niqab* of recent development which some urban women wear as part of the *zayy Islami* ('Islamic dress').

SAFSAAFA AND THE GENERAL

Radwa Ashour

I

'The general has sent for you,' my colleague whispered, the telegram in his outstretched hand. Standing in the tent adjoining the stage, we spoke in low tones. We couldn't see either the actors or the children spread across the bare ground of the cul-de-sac, but we could hear the dialogue, the murmurings and the comments.

'Let us seek the ruling of the queen!'

I set the gilded pasteboard crown on my head and waited until the second actor repeated the phrase: 'Yes, let us seek the ruling of the queen!' I mounted the four steps leading on to the stage, which had originally been the back of a flatbed lorry.

I took my position, standing between my two colleagues, and gazed down at the gaunt faces before me, at the shining eyes that were staring at me as they applauded. I made a slight bow, returning their greetings, and we resumed the performance.

KAMEL: Your majesty, I did not betray this man in his absence. I protected his home and supported his wife and children. But when he returned, your majesty, instead of a welcoming embrace and tears of gratitude he wanted to kill me. He is an unbeliever, my sovereign queen, he is full of spite and rancour, and his heart is as corrupt and foul as rotting fruit.

ABDALLAH: Liar! He is lying, your majesty. Hear my words: I will tell you the whole story. One day, Kamel came to me and said: 'Abdallah, I have some good news for you. Do you see that high mountain? If you go to the foot of it, climb to the summit, descend the other side and walk along the road you'll come upon an old woman who has golden baskets. If you greet her, she will give you one of them. They are magic baskets, Abdallah. You drop a penny there, you find a hundred pennies in its place; you put a loaf of bread inside, you get a hundred loaves instead.'

THE QUEEN: Did you say that to him, Kamel?

KAMEL: Yes, my sovereign queen. I said it to him.

ABDALLAH: He said it, and I believed it. Leaving my land, my home and my children behind, I went. Seven years, your majesty – seven years of searching. My shoes wore out, cracks filled the soles of my feet and my eyesight grew weak. Sadness built its nest in my heart. Seven years, walking alone, with no son on whom I could lean, with no wife to give companionship to the desolation of my days. Seven years, and I found nothing. Nothing at all.

KAMEL: Because you're an ass, and that's not my fault!

ABDALLAH: My sovereign queen, Kamel deceived me, and then he robbed me. I returned home and what do you think I found?

KAMEL: You found that I had brought up the children and cultivated the land and added another storey to the house. Do you deny it?

ABDALLAH: I returned and found that he had taken my land, my house, my wife and my children.

THE QUEEN: And what do you want now, Abdallah?

ABDALLAH: I want him to get out of my house and to pay me compensation for the clothes I wore out, for this body of mine which has grown old and for my heart that now droops like a wilted flower.

KAMEL: He's raving, your majesty.

THE QUEEN: Reconciliation is a blessing, Abdallah, and it is the best path to follow. Peace is one of the graces of Allah, Kamel. You are brothers. Love each other, and cooperate for your own good.

KAMEL and ABDALLAH (in unison):   How?!

THE QUEEN: Abdallah, you help Kamel to farm the land, and Kamel, you give Abdallah food and shelter.

ABDALLAH: This is unjust!

KAMEL: It's impossible! He wanted to *murder* me, my sovereign liege. How can I allow him to live in my own house?

THE QUEEN: Give him a hut in the field.

KAMEL: No, that I cannot do!

ABDALLAH: He robbed me of everything I had. He absolutely must return all that he stole and pay me compensation.

KAMEL: I didn't steal a thing. The land has become mine because I have cultivated it. The house has come into my possession because I enlarged it and added another storey. The wife and children are my right because I have fed and cared for them.

THE QUEEN: Love each other. Live together. Conciliation is a benefit and a blessing. This is my ruling. Do you not accept it?

KAMEL AND ABDALLAH (in unison):   No, we do not accept it! (They turn to face the audience). Do *you* accept it?

THE CHILDREN: No! We don't accept it!

KAMEL, ABDALLAH and THE QUEEN: Then what is the solution?

Tonight, as on the previous evenings, the children were like kernels of maize in a skillet, jumping up and hopping around in enthusiasm. Their eyes had grown wide, their necks were craned forward and their hands shot up, requesting the right to speak.

A boy with a shock of curly hair, skin the colour of wheat and green eyes got to his feet. He was wearing a vertically striped *gallabiyya* that accentuated his thinness and revealed his protruding rib cage.

'At midday, when Kamel has gone to sleep under the tree, Abdallah should tie . . .'. The children broke in, protesting, for they could not hear him clearly. The boy started again, speaking more loudly and at a slower pace.

'At midday, when Kamel has gone to sleep in the field under the tree, Abdallah should tie him to the tree trunk and leave him there to starve. Then he'll realize he's wrong, and that Allah is the Truth.* And Abdallah shouldn't untie him until he repents and says "I'll never do it again." '

'This kind of talk won't do!' shouted another young boy. 'I have a better solution.' This youth was round-faced with large and beautiful black eyes and thick, pitch-black hair. I asked him to stand up so that he could present his solution

'I *am* standing up!' he replied, in a tone of protest.

The children laughed. He didn't join in, but tried to silence them so they would listen to what he had to say.

'Abdallah can hide in the maize until Kamel comes by. Then he can shoot him. If he does that, he'll be saved from Kamel and so will we, because Kamel is a thief and a liar and he betrayed the trust Abdallah put in him!'

'I have another answer.' It was a third child, repeating the phrase over and over without a pause as he raised both hands. He was very dark with delicate features and a small, slight form. His almond-shaped eyes shone with a sly glint reiterated in a grin that he was trying hard to conceal. He stood up to speak. His shirt was stretched tightly over his chest, despite the slenderness of his body, as if the garment belonged to a younger brother or was a shirt he himself had worn two or three years before.

'Kamel is wrong,' he said. 'Abdallah is wrong too. And the Queen is wrong.' He paused for just a moment, giving his mates a look, as if to make sure that they understood what he had just said.

'Kamel is a thief,' he went on. 'He doesn't safeguard either others' rights or a friend. Right?'

'Right!' shouted the children, agreeing fully with his words.

'And Abdallah is an idiot because he left his land and house and children to go and search for a strange, marvellous basket which only exists in the tales of el-Shatir Hasan.* Correct?'

'Correct!' The children were nodding as they echoed him.

'As for the Queen, she has weighted the two sides unevenly, because she is making the one who has rights equal to the one who plunders those rights. OK so far?'

'OK!'

The boy laughed and the infection spread to the little ones, who began to giggle.

'The solution is for Abdallah to be turned into a donkey, because he is one. And the Queen should be turned into a black cat without a shadow, whom people will shun because she is an evil spirit. And Kamel should be turned into a scorpion, a yellow one. And the entire story of the donkey, the black cat and the yellow scorpion should be included in our primary school reader so we can all benefit from it.'

By now the children were stirred up. They surged forward and milled about enthusiastically, screaming with laughter and tossing out exuberant shouts.

'Why has the general sent for me?' I asked myself as I walked down the narrow alley leading to the house of Umm Ahmad, with whom I stay as a guest. I knocked on the door, and she opened it without asking who it was, for she knew the sound of my footsteps and always recognized my knock.

We sat down next to each other on the floor matting. Umm Ahmad sat cross-legged, not supporting herself on

anything. She was cleaning the gas burner, preparing to
make tea for us as I leant my back against the wall and
extended my legs, rubbing them because they hurt.

'The general sent for me today.'

'Why? – Allah protect us from all evil.'

There was nothing I could say.

'News that costs today, tomorrow will be for free!' As
she intoned the proverb, she went on working at the
burner to unblock it.

'Think I should go?'

'What can you possibly lose?' Having succeeded in
lighting the burner she put the navy-blue enamelled
teapot on the flame before speaking again. 'You won't
lose anything by it. How was the performance tonight?'

Umm Ahmad always wakes up before sunrise, collects
the dung from the animal pen, does the milking,
transports the big earthenware water-jars and bakes
bread to order for her acquaintances and neighbours to
buy. Then she returns from her morning errands to find
me still asleep. She awakens me, always with the same
phrase: 'Your mosquito-net is dark blue!* You've
certainly been sleeping soundly: it's almost time for the
noon call to prayer!' I look at my watch and discover
that it's no later than ten o'clock.

When Umm Ahmad came back today she found me
sitting on the mat, combing my hair as I waited for her to
return.

'Your meeting with the general is all they're talking
about in town.'

'Who let the news out?'

'Didn't the telegram reach you via the police station?
How could the whole town *not* know?'

I went on plaiting my hair as Umm Ahmad prepared
two glasses of tea so we could have them together as was
our habit every morning.

'The women are going to call after the noon prayers,
and the men will come by after the evening prayers.'

'Do they still have any hopes in the general?' I spoke without raising my head, as I dipped a bit of bread into my tea.

'It's not a question of hope now. It *is* a try, though. What can we lose?'

It was close to midnight by the time the house emptied of people. Umm Ahmad had cleaned the burner and relit it over and over, with hardly a pause, offering the visitors her hospitality.

When everyone had gone away there sat before me a large pile of paper, sheets of various sizes written with fountain pens and ballpoints and pencils and copypens: petitions, complaints and claims of unjust treatment, requests and just plain letters.

Umm Ahmad brought over her ancient black shawl and bound all of the letters up into a bundle which she knotted tightly and precisely. She took three bread rolls from the large basket and tied them up in a handkerchief, muttering, 'It's a long trip.'

'Are you going to travel in that dress?' she asked.

'The other one has a rip in it.'

'Go to bed now. There's plenty of time – we'll sleep on it.'

She woke me up at dawn. I discovered that she had borrowed a black velvet *gallabiyya* and a blue cotton shawl for me. I put on the *gallabiyya*, placed the shawl over my head, and picked up the large bundle with my right hand, carrying the little one in my other hand. We left the house.

Two of my colleagues and three youths from the village were waiting to accompany us to the railway station. It was hard to make out their faces at that violet hour, but I knew who they were anyway. On the way, we met others whom I didn't know, men and women who had come to accompany us too. By the time we left the village, walking along the river road that would take us into town, where the railway station was located, we had become a procession. The marching feet stirred up

the dust and the clamour grew so loud that it drowned
out the chirping of the birds.

We reached the station and stood waiting. The early
morning fog had lifted and everything was clearly
visible, sharply outlined in the strong sunlight: the name
of the little town on a large sign over the platform; the
brown faces, thin bodies, bare feet.

The train came into view, filling the air with puffs of
smoke. The voices of those who had come to see me off
rose, their words and phrases mingling, superimposed
one upon the other.

'*Sitt* Safsaafa, we're entrusting you with this, we're
counting on you to report everything!'

'Inflation has done us in.'

'Water's short.'

'The electricity's been cut off.'

'The children are ailing from so much walking in the
winter and in the summer sun – the trip to school is a real
voyage!'

'The hospital's at the other end of the world.'

'Sitt Safsaafa, we're counting on you – don't forget!'

'So long now, have a safe journey!'

I had turned to put my foot on the steps into the train
carriage when I heard them calling out to me. I looked
round and saw them – two little shapes, panting from
the distance they had run, their faces and hair damp
with sweat.

'Hey, Sitt Safsaafa, don't you remember me?'

It was the dark, slim boy who had suggested that
Kamel be transformed into a yellow scorpion. I answered
him with a smile.

'Of course I remember you!'

'I want a box of coloured pencils! And this is my
friend, he wants an orange. Will you forget?'

'I won't forget.'

II

'What does the general want from me?'

A bouquet of roses with a card bearing his name had preceded him. Then he had arrived. That was the first time I had seen him in person. He was wearing a blue naval uniform decorated with white embroidered lotus flowers. His hands were covered by delicate white gloves made of a fine, soft leather, and he was grasping a slender ebony cane with a gold top. He was short and thin, his face hairless and round, his pale complexion infused with a light reddish tinge. His fine, straight, chestnut-coloured hair was arranged carefully and parted on the left. He sat down, his legs together and his back ramrod-straight in the manner of soldiers, and he talked confidently and easily.

He told me I had the presence of the sea and the delicacy of a butterfly. He said that my form, my facial features and my plaited hair, my height and upright carriage all reminded him of that exquisite statue of the peasant woman which stands atop the green hill, overlooking the entrance to the capital.

'In sum, you are magnificent,' he said. 'Your theatrical delivery is unique and I am a true admirer of yours.'

Tapping his cane loudly against the floor to announce the end of the visit, he left.

A month later I received another bouquet of roses, a larger one this time. Then he came to propose marriage to me.

'Are you refusing because I'm already married?' he asked. 'Or is it because of that boy people say you go out with? The lad is a nobody. He's absolutely nothing. A mere director of plays, known only to a handful of people who have a special interest in the theatre. But you – you are young, pretty and talented. When I marry you, you'll become the general's wife. Do you know what being The General's Wife means?'

He tapped his cane on the floor exactly as he had done
on the previous visit, but this time he did not smile as he
extended his hand to shake mine. It was then, as he left,
that I noticed the lameness in his walk.

The next day, Yusuf came to see me.

'What did he want?'

'Marriage!'

'Did you accept?'

'I turned him down.'

'Will you agree to marry me?'

'Am I suitable for you?'

He burst out laughing. 'You're crazy!'

I almost told him that I loved him and wanted him
and desired him and needed him. 'But you're still
Yusuf,' I nearly said. 'Yusuf, who reads books and
travels on aeroplanes and speaks to important people as
if he were one of them. You're Yusuf, and I'm Safsaafa,'
I almost said to him. 'Safsaafa, daughter of a father who
lived and died barefoot, who never bought a pair of
shoes in his life. And perhaps, had he been able to buy
shoes he would not have found a pair the size of his rough
feet, which knew only the feel of the soil in the fields and
the dust of the road.'

But all I said was: 'Yusuf, I'm *not* suitable for you!'

The train let out a high whistle that was followed
immediately by a sharp, long screech, produced by the
friction of the wheels against the rails as the train slowed
down more and more. It was running parallel to the
station platform now; it came to a stop. Passengers got
off and others boarded. Another whistle, announcing
the resumption of the journey.

'I wonder why the general wants me?'

Forty years have passed since that first meeting. I was
nineteen at the time and he was forty or more. 'My star
is ascendant and you are marvellous, radiant as a
butterfly,' he said. I laughed at his odd choice of words,
but I was afraid, and I wanted him to leave. He went
away.

Two years later I married Yusuf. Whenever we were rehearsing a new production he would fling his instructions at me, yelling and scolding. I would react with fury, and the two of us were like a pair of mountain goats, horns interlocking as they butted. I did love him though. He loved me too, and we both loved the theatre – its velvety curtain, its stage, the lights, the terror of opening nights and the glistening tears through which we would see the audience, standing up to applaud wildly for us at the end of the evening. It was all splendid and captivating, giving us confidence and strength and also something that was gentle and dazzling, like the bouquets of roses which we received after the performance. Those roses were beautiful, and their radiance was enhanced by the shine of the cellophane and the thin coloured bands of ribbon tied around the wrapping and stems.

Then Yusuf went away. He left without a word, without even a farewell kiss. I slapped my face in grief and tore my clothes, all the while repeating, 'Yusuf deceived me, he left me, how could he?'

Holding me, they said the same words, time and time again: 'And when has a human being ever taken his leave at the moment of death? Death snatched him away, he didn't choose it, and only God has power and strength!'

The general sent a telegram of condolence, a purple wreath, and a personal representative to the funeral. A few days later he came in person to see me. The house was filled with guards and escorts.

'Let me offer my condolences,' he said.

'We have lost a major artist,' he said.

'God bless him and all of us,' he said. And then he tapped his cane against the floor.

Three months later he came again, but this time his escorts and guards remained outside the flat.

'The mourning period* is over now, isn't it?' he asked, his demeanour severe and his eyes empty of expression.

He was wearing his usual military uniform and grasping the ebony cane. A broad smile that revealed all his teeth – as well as some gaps where teeth had been extracted – took me by surprise.

'I knew you would agree.'

'Agree to what?'

'To our marriage.'

'Have I?'

'Haven't you?'

His lips tightened and his expression grew even sterner, as he tapped his cane on the floor. He got to his feet and walked away with his slow, heavy, lame walk, while his retinue and guards scurried ahead – to the lift, the stairs, the motor car, the streets.

The train let out a sharp, broken whistle and took off, paying no heed to whatever was behind. Through the window the fields ran as if competing in a race, as if they were slightly mad, running either like the hunter or the hunted.

'I wonder what the general wants from me?'

I opened Umm Ahmad's handkerchief and took out a bit of bread. I ate it and knotted the handkerchief over what remained.

After that last visit I had seen him only once. A few years had passed, and I was standing on the stage, returning people's salutations after the close of the performance. They were applauding as I bobbed my head towards them and smiled. It was then that I caught sight of him. He was sitting by himself in the front row, surrounded by empty seats to left and right. I saw him, and then, as if for the first time, I saw the others sitting behind him. They filled the red velveteen seats, the men in dark suits, white shirts and coloured silk neckties, and the women in evening dresses, their hair done carefully and their eyes drawn skilfully. I saw them, and then I took in the ceiling overlaid with gold leaf, the boxes with their figured walls and the crystal clusters dangling from lighted chandeliers. I saw it all, and then suddenly I saw it no more. For a fleeting moment the place looked entirely empty to me, empty except for the general sitting alone in his blue military uniform and white leather gloves, leaning forward with both hands resting on the top of his cane.

When I walked out of the theatre I knew that I was leaving it for the last time. I had given no thought to where I might go after that or on what stage I would stand, but I was certain that this time I had left their theatre for good.

'Why does the general want me?'

The train went on, its speed unchanged, bisecting the farmland that lay to either side, but I knew now that it was drawing near to the station that was my destination. For this place gave off the smell of moisture, with its tinge of iodine, and cold breezes were slapping gently against my face. The surging noise of the sea was filling my ears, not because I could hear it - for the noise made by the train swallowed everything else - but because the smell and the breeze were carrying it to me, so that my eyes could see its blueness billowing, rising and exploding.

III

I held out the telegram to the officer, who took it and began to riffle through a file folder. He stopped at a particular page and looked at me, scrutinizing my face, then at the folder and then at my face again.

'Please come along.'

Two of the armed guards accompanied me to a dark room, its heavy gloom broken only by incandescent buttons of yellow, red and green. 'Walk two steps forward and stop,' said someone whose position I couldn't exactly make out in the darkness. I stopped. The contents of my body and the large bundle, and Umm Ahmad's bread in the knotted kerchief, appeared on a television screen.

I left the room in the company of the two guards. We entered a broad, tiled courtyard walled in by a towering stone wall along which, at equal intervals, were planted orange trees. The stone wall had the darkness of ancient prison doorways; the trees, which had small trunks and fragile branches, were heavy with oranges that appeared and disappeared among the abundant green leaves.

We crossed the courtyard and came to a narrow corridor that cut through a sand-coloured building shaped like a rectangular box. We entered and then were outside again. From the end of the drive the ancient fortress stared at us, a heavily fortified edifice that obstructed the view of the sea beyond.

Once inside, we came to a spacious hall decorated with Persian carpets. The walls were covered with huge mirrors, each one framed in silver inlaid with gold. From the ceiling hung enormous chandeliers, whole grape-clusters of crystal. I was invited to lunch at the general's table.

The guards conducted me to my designated place, where I found a card bearing my name. Four invitees, none of whom I knew, had arrived before me. The tables were arranged in a semicircle so that once seated the guests could see the musicians before them.

The music opened with the military anthem. The guests rose to their feet, eyes directed toward the band. I looked: the general was standing in a closed glass stall set above the musicians' space. His chestnut hair had disappeared, leaving in its place a shining globe. He was no longer thin: the stoutness he had acquired since I had seen him last made him look even shorter than before.

The general moved his head slightly to right and left. The guests clapped and called out. He smiled and then sat down at his table, alone and set apart behind the glass partition. The guests sat down.

Men and women in embroidered clothes began coming and going with obvious energy, carrying vessels of food: soup, fish, meat, vegetables, sweet stuffed pancakes, other sweets and fruit. Afterwards the men went round pouring Arabic coffee from gold-coloured pitchers while the women offered cigarettes from wooden boxes inlaid with mother-of-pearl.

All of this activity was accompanied by the performance of musical pieces, solo and in concert, the melodies mingling with the striking of the golden spoons against china plates and the sounds of soup being sipped, meat being chewed and fruit chomped, someone belching and someone else blowing his nose.

Faces were glistening with beads of sweat, teeth chewing furiously, breathing becoming heavier, eyes fixed on the general sitting in his glass cage and eating alone.

'I wonder why the general wants me?'

I followed the two guards into a dark narrow passageway. The light from the lemon-yellow lamps at first seemed very faint after the vast, chandelier-lit hall. We started up a narrow spiral staircase in one of the towers. Because the staircase was so cramped the guards could not continue walking on either side of me; one went ahead of me and the other followed behind. We ascended without a single pause, until I felt the sweat trickling from my neck and forehead and seeping through the roots of my hair. My breathing was growing heavier and my knees started aching. I stopped for a moment's rest and they halted too. I leant on the edge of an opening in the stone wall. I gazed out across the iron bars and saw the sea below us, its blueness rising in a blaze of light and colour, surging on to the shore defiantly, colliding against the breakwaters, striking the granite and causing the spray to rush forward and upward in all directions: countless tiny seagulls embroidering the sky with their whiteness.

My face was dripping with sweat from the cramped space of the tower and its stifling humidity. We resumed our climb, going on until we reached a small waiting room. I sat down between the guards and stayed until I was called.

I entered a vast hall and saw the general, sitting on a white couch, silk-covered pillows in bright colours surrounding him. He was wearing his usual military uniform.

When I had drawn quite near he rose to meet me. He walked towards me with his halting and uneven gait, leaning on his gold and ebony cane. He appeared to have aged greatly, for wrinkles covered his face.

'Safsaafa?' he asked as he shook my hand and smiled, revealing an even, regular row of shining teeth and a pair of rosy, clear gums. He gave a sudden laugh which revealed that his voice had become faint and hoarse, like that of an invalid.

'You've changed a lot; you look quite worn and tattered. Are you really Safsaafa?' He invited me to sit down on the chair nearest to the sofa.

'Next year the country will celebrate the fiftieth anniversary of my guardianship,' said the general. 'It will be the people's festival. They will dance and sing, they will slaughter the feastday lambs and scatter rice and wheat and flowers, and the river of their love for me will overflow its banks in every village and city.'

He smiled delightedly, and I noticed that his teeth were false. He went on.

'The anniversary of my accession is an occasion for the people. My gift to them, to mark their festival, will be my presence – for I will go to them. The general, in flesh and blood, will descend from the fortress so that the people can see him with their own eyes and rejoice. What a gift. *What* a gift!'

He closed his eyes. When he opened them again they were covered with a film of tears. 'And you, Safsaafa – you will come with me. I will take you with me to the people, because they love you. Is it true that they love you?'

He stared at me sharply and directly, frowning and moving his lips quickly and suddenly as if wanting to extract remnants of food from between his teeth. Then his face grew still. He became calmer, closed his eyes and went on.

'For fifty years I have been working in the service of the people. I have watched over their interests, carried their burdens and marked out their path. I have protected them even from themselves whenever evil has threatened them. For fifty years I have concerned myself entirely with the people, neglecting nothing, never letting up and never resting. Alone I have carried this responsibility under which even mountains would collapse. I am a mountain, Safsaafa, a strange and miraculous mountain, a mountain with a good heart. . . . But the responsibility is a very heavy burden. I have thought long and hard about bringing others in to share it with me, but I have always pulled back, for who can vouchsafe to me their loyalty to the people? Who can guarantee their love and loyalty? I love the people. Where will I find anyone who has the same deep and abiding love?'

The general was now going on as if speaking to himself, or to the walls, in a faint, hoarse, trembling voice.

'They are my sons and daughters. Children. They differ, they quarrel, they fight, and I, as their father, bring them together and assemble them as one would string a necklace. Like a hen I tuck them in under my wing. Like a mother wolf I defend and protect them. I am their merciful father, their tender mother, their vigilant protector, their sheltering umbrella. I am their cloudless and serene sky, and their radiant sun, I . . .'

'I'm leaving now!'

He didn't hear me. He was wholly absorbed in his own words, his eyes closed and his features quivering, stirred up by what he was saying. He looked as if he were about to burst into tears as he sat there facing me, his lax shoulders drooping, his chest and stomach resting on his large rear. Since his feet did not reach the floor his skinny legs dangled in the air as if they belonged to a child or a doll.

'I'm leaving.'

But he paid no attention. I picked up my bundle and Umm Ahmad's handkerchief and went out. I found the two guards waiting for me outside the reception room. We crossed the inner courtyard, went through the narrow corridor, and then walked across the outer courtyard. Finally I found myself alone on the main road.

I headed towards the sea. When I reached it I squatted down on the sand and watched the waves surging and rising, covering the beach only to withdraw again from the sandy shore which was now wet, soft and dark. The scattering spray touched me; the surging sea wrapped itself around me and filled my chest with that smell which has no like. I followed the circling of the gulls as they flew away from the water only to come back to it again. And other birds, smaller ones, fluttered past quickly, strongly, determinedly.

It was Yusuf who had first taken me to the sea. When I saw it I ran to it, opening my arms; I ran away, and then ran back to it. I laughed until the tears ran down my cheeks; I danced around. I walked into the water; it covered me to the waist.

'You are a water nymph!' said Yusuf.

'I'm Safsaafa!' I said.

'You're a water nymph. You have the tail of a fish . . . Look – where have your legs gone?'

Every time Yusuf requested that we leave, I demanded that we stay until we saw the water glinting like a pearl with the golden colour of the sunset and the silvery tones of twilight. The moon appeared, a thin crescent, like a fine yellow line drawn by a pencil upon a pure surface of bold blue.

Yusuf spoke. 'This crescent moon is me . . . and you are that blazing disc that has just disappeared into the sea.'

I laughed but he did not. When midnight came we were still sitting before the sea, watching it: the tumult of its waves, their regular rhythm roaring around us, and the spray that touched our faces so gently.

I wiped my palm across my face. It was wet, with spray or tears. Yusuf had been the first to bring me here; that I would never forget. But now it was time to return. I uncovered my head and rolled up my sleeves. I took off my shoes and my feet touched the soft freshness of the moist sand. I walked into the water, and when I reached it I bent over, filled my palm, and began to wash myself. When I had finished I headed for the main road. My face, feet, hands and the edges of my gown were wet with sea water. My right hand clutched Umm Ahmad's shawl tied round the letters that people had given me, and my eyes searched for a shop where I could buy coloured pencils and an orange for the boys.

NOTES

Title note: 'Safsaafa wa'l-jiniral', published in Egypt in *Adab wa-Naqd*, no. 35, January 1988, pp. 65–79, and in the Lebanese journal *al-Tariq*, vol. 47, no. 1, March 1988, pp. 170–82.

Allah is the Truth: a phrase in colloquial Egyptian Arabic when someone recognizes that he/she has done something wrong. It links wrongdoing to the idea of straying from one's religion.

The tales of el-Shatir Hasan: 'Clever Hasan', legendary hero of tales of fantasy told to children. (See Etidal Osman's story 'A House for Us'.)

Your mosquito-net is dark blue: said when someone sleeps late in the morning and/or soundly.

the mourning period: the three months of mourning required of widows, according to Islamic practice, before they can remarry.

I SAW THE DATE-PALMS

Radwa Ashour

It had been a long winter and I could make myself wait
no longer. I put on my old overcoat, wound my woollen
scarf round my head and went outside. After passing
through several streets I reached the trees. I looked them
over, checking each one closely. When my eyes found
nothing on the dry boughs, I reached out to run my
hand along the branches, probing them with care.
Sometimes my hands would stop and my heartbeat
would quicken; then I would discover that what I felt
was not what I was looking for but just a knot on a
dried-out branch. I was confident, though, that I would
find them – the stiff, tiny, globular buds.

The colour deceives you at first. You think it is
nothing, but if you look carefully you will find that it is a
bud. Its greyness is not really grey, nor is its dry touch
really dryness. If you go on watching it, and if you wait,
it will enlarge and open, revealing its hidden greenness
to you.

I was searching for just such a bud when one of my
colleagues caught sight of me.

'Fawzia,' he called, 'what are you doing out in the
street in this accursed cold, when everyone else is indoors
at home?'

'I'm searching for buds,' I replied.

'God, Fawzia, you're mad!'

He was joking. I remember clearly the laughing tone in his voice and the warm, friendly look in his eyes.

And at the end of a day spent searching I returned home unsuccessful, asking myself, 'How long will it be?' It was then that I remembered the cactus plant which my aunt Fatima had brought me from our home town. I had set it next to the front door and forgotten all about it. When I remembered it, I told myself that it must have died, for I had not watered it in several months. I went to have a look at it anyway. The soil had dried out completely, cracking and becoming the colour of blond coffee beans. The stem was dry and yellowish, although it showed new growth. The needle-edged blades were unchanged: rising broadly where they separated from the trunk, they became thin and pointed as they opened and arched downwards. My aunt's cactus stood straight and green on its stalk. I watered it.

I came to love planting and I began to plant things – in a clay pot, in an empty tin, in a glass. Anything that would do for planting I filled with earth. At the proper depth, I'd implant a fruit stone or infix a green shoot, and then I would water the soil.

In those days no one said I was insane. But later they said so – on the day they brought me news of my cousin's death.

'Your cousin has died, Fawzia.'

'Died?'

I asked them to wait so that I could accompany them to offer my condolences. They saw me squat before them, fill an empty tin with soil and fix a sweet basil shoot within. I steadied it by pressing my fist down repeatedly on the dirt so that it would hold the shoot fast, embracing it until soil and shoot were intertwined. I inundated it with water.

'Now we can go,' I said.

I saw them slapping their palms together in pity –

they found my behaviour so strange – and I heard them saying, 'Fawzia has gone mad – may God compensate us for her madness!' I didn't understand why they had said this, and I was even more surprised when I heard one of them whisper, 'Fawzia is imitating rich folk who decorate their homes with plants!'

I was surprised because the speaker is from our village, and he knows. We are peasants. It is true that the women of our Upper Egyptian family do not go out into the fields to till the soil, but farming is their life. They open their eyes upon farming, and – at the moment of death – close their eyes upon it too. And I remember that our house in the village had a mint plant on its roof; inside there was a cactus and at the door a date-palm. I remember that my father – God rest his soul – used to say that the date-palm is a blessed tree; with it the Lord graced His servants, and by mentioning it in the Qur'an He bestowed honour upon it. And my father said that the Prophet – God's blessings be upon him — said: 'Honour your paternal aunts the date-palms.' And that he called them our 'paternal aunts' because they were created from the extra clay left over after the creation of Adam, and that they resemble human beings. They were created male and female, tall and straight of stature, palm cores growing on their tops like the brain of a human being in his head. Should evil afflict that core, the date-palm would perish.

My father used to entrust the date-palms to my brother's care, just as my mother charged me every dawn (as she gave me her daily instructions for sweeping the house and feeding the chickens) with watering the mint plant. Whenever I forgot – and I was always in a hurry, since I did these daily chores before leaving for school – she got angry, and would raise her voice and scold me.

'Shame on you, my girl, this is a bad omen! May the Lord give your father long life and give our home prosperity.'

But God did not extend either his life or hers. Even my two brothers departed, and I became – after moving to Cairo and settling here – like an orphaned branch severed from its tree. And it seemed I had forgotten the mint, the cactus, the date-palm and everything.

Then my aunt Fatima, my father's sister, came to visit me. She pressed me to her bosom, weeping over the ruination of our House, whose light had gone out and whose cactus plant had dried up. She restrained her tears and sat down crosslegged on the Assiuti rug to open the basket that she had brought with her.

'I brought you some bread I've baked and dates from your papa's palm-tree, and I broke off a branch from the cactus in our home so that you could have it.'

As my aunt passed the cactus cutting across to me, she went on speaking, tears still in her eyes.

'The cactus in our house was a cutting that my mother broke off from her own plant the day I got married and moved to my husband's house. So this is from your grandmother's cactus, from your grand-mother's grandmother's cactus. God bless you, Fawzia, my daughter, and make your home prosperous.'

My aunt had reminded me. And when I remembered, I began to plant things. And people said I was insane.

At work, too, they whisper together behind my back. Once a colleague said to me, 'Fawzia, look at your hands.'

I understood that she was referring to the black lines under my fingernails. 'This isn't filth,' I said. 'It's mud left over from my planting.'

She patted me on the shoulder. 'It isn't proper, not at all proper for a government employee.'

I don't understand what offends my colleagues when I grow plants. The place where we work is gloomy and ancient. Bits of paint are always falling off the walls, spiders have woven their webs in the corners and insects have made their nests. And I am certain that rats have their lairs here. At evening they leave their dens, roaming all night among the offices with nothing to restrain them. Every day I thank God that they haven't yet chewed up any of the papers in the files in my custody (those old grey files ranged on wooden shelves that are worn half away, their original colour hard to fathom). And even the long rectangular space that extends along the façade of the building – we call this space the garden – is flooded by the overflow from the sewers. We can't even enter or leave the building without walking very cautiously along five adjacent stones that form a bridge to the doorstep.

I was not remiss with my colleagues. When I realized what the conditions were like where I work, I planted three shrubs of Indian jasmine at home and tended them carefully. When they had grown and the leaves were thick on their branches, I carried them to the office and placed them side by side on the building's only balcony. But my colleagues paid no attention to the jasmine's beauty, even when the bushes produced blossoms, although they did pay attention to the dirt under my fingernails.

At work they don't understand me, and in my neighbourhood, too, I heard them with my own ears talking about 'mad Fawzia who throws herself on date stones as if they are golden guineas'. My behaviour astonishes them, and theirs amazes me. When any of them eats a date and spits out the stone, he'll spit it so that it falls at a distance, or he spits it into his hand first and then tosses it away with a full swing of his arm so that it lands even further away. I run to pick it up and I hide it in my deep pocket. When I get home, I place it on a piece of dampened cotton and leave it for four or five days, tending it each day and following its progress as it swells and grows soft, until I can touch its freshness and I know that the time is near. Soon after, I bury it in soil and saturate it with water. And then I wait.

I have wished that my home had a lot of space; I have wished it were surrounded by ground that I could cultivate. It saddens me that my home consists of only one room and a single balcony which is so small and narrow that it doesn't even provide enough space for everything I grow. I used to put my flowerpots on the balcony wall but I stopped doing that because the children on my street kept throwing stones at them. The first time I found a flowerpot shattered and the shoot planted within broken, its leaves wilted, I thought of them, but I repeated to myself the proverb that says: 'To think even a little evil of someone is a sin.'

When the incident recurred my suspicions were confirmed, and even more so when the children began bothering me as I was coming home carrying a tin or two – large ones of the kind used to preserve white cheese or olives. Amm Mitwalli the grocer used to give them to me so that I could use them as planters. But when he realized that I wasn't buying perfumed soap or imported cheese in silver and gold wrappers he became irritated and would no longer give me the tins, despite my assurances to him that I can't buy these items from him, or from anyone else either, because they are expensive and my salary is meagre.

Whenever Amm Mitwalli gave me the tins, the boys would walk behind me, chanting a processional for me, their voices like solemn chimes:

> The madwoman's coming back
> Clutching a tin in her hands
> She's got no mind
> She's got no brains
> A *falso* brain and a mind of tin!

Their behaviour grieved me; I felt a tightening in my throat and I wanted to cry. Instead, I leant over to pick up the first stone in my path and I hurled it in their direction, all the while swearing at them out loud.

On one of these occasions, Umm Sulayman – that heavy woman with the gold tooth – materialized suddenly before me. Hands on her ample hips, she blocked my way.

'I am sorry, Sitt Umm Sulayman,* I didn't intend any harm, but your son Sulayman and the other boys were swearing at me and insulting me,' I said to her in my own defence. 'Also, Sitt Umm Sulayman, yesterday they broke the planter that I had put next to the front door.'

Her laugh startled me but I went on, 'Umm Sulayman, you consider yourself responsible for watching over Sulayman and protecting him, isn't that so? Consider me a mother too – I'm a mother of plants!'

Umm Sulayman wiggled her eyebrows and a raspy voice came scraping from her throat: 'Congratulations on the birth of your *zar*', your plants, Umm Zar'! May you have a long life and bear many more!'

She turned her back on me and walked away, resuming her fearful, high laughter.

I found no one to whom I could complain except Papa Muhammad, who is a hired hand at the plant nursery and lives in a wooden shack right at his workplace. When we first got to know each other, I called him Amm Muhammad and he called me Sitt Fawzia, and when we became friends, I began to call him Papa Muhammad and he named me Umm Ahmad, after my father, God rest his soul, whose name was Ahmad. When the world starts closing in on me, I go to him and talk. This time I complained about Umm Sulayman and he advised me to insult her just as she had insulted me.

'I'll try,' I told him, and I returned home. But I wasn't sure that I could do it, because Umm Sulayman has scared me so much that I see her in my dreams, laughing until her teeth show, long and frightening, especially that gleaming gold tooth. I see her laughing and the dream becomes a nightmare.

But not all my dreams are nightmares. When I am untroubled, I see the fields and then my dreams are beautiful, like dreams should be . . . and they're in colour. When I see a field of wheat, it looks to me like pure gold, the ears of wheat undulating, bending and billowing in a sea of saffron.

When I see a field of maize, the cobs are already mature on their stalks, their tufts a winey red. The field, although green, looks brownish red like the waters of the Nile in the ninth month,* heavy with silt, before the coming of the floods.

And when it is an orange grove that appears, I see the trees looking small and rotund and weighted down with fruit, like the women of our village. Against the green of the branches the oranges show off their colour, and in the blue heights the sun mirrors them.

When the plants are still concealed, I see the earth between moisture and dryness stretching out free and black, the seeds hiding within, except for a few which have split their shells and sent out their shoots of green.

Once only I saw the date-palms, a grove in the early morning. The sun had not yet risen but was about to, and was already dying the violet horizon with the colour of henna. I saw the date-palms, lots of them, straight and towering. In them I saw the faces of my family, my father and mother and aunt and cousin. Their faces were green, pale with the hue of the palm leaves. But I could not tell for sure whether they were standing behind the trunks or whether the trunks were behind them. I heard a mellow, warm voice. It sounded like the voice of a Qur'an-reciter chanting holy verses before the dawn call to prayer, or like something else, I really don't know. But the voice rang out, echoing across the date-palm grove in the moments before dawn, and I told myself, 'Fawzia, you are at the gates, so prepare yourself.'

But then I awoke. I opened my eyes and found only the picture which hung on the old wall, and I knew it had been a dream. A tear rolled from my eye; then I pulled myself together and got up.

Today a woman who lives on my street came to see me. She said she had seen the flowerpots on my balcony and she told me they were pretty. She asked me shyly if I could teach her. So I showed her how, I gave her a mint sprig that I had planted, and then we sat and talked.

NOTES

Title note: 'Ra'aytu al-nakhl', published in *Adab wa-naqd*, no. 29, February 1987, pp. 27–32.

Umm Sulayman: 'mother of Sulayman'; calling parents by the names of their oldest children is a common practice.

the ninth month: September, the month when the annual flooding of the Nile (before the Aswan High Dam was constructed) reached its height; a time of fertility.

THINGS CAST DOWN ON
THE ROAD ARE LOST

Sahar Tawfiq

'Don't wake up, or else you might see me stealing,' she said to the dead body lying on the floor of the empty room.

She sat down beside the dead body. She clasped her arms round her knees. She looked at it warily. 'I know I have lost this thing that you left me,' she said. 'That's why you are coming to me now.'

Yesterday I was there. 'This box was for me,' I said to her.

'No, it's for me,' she said. 'And you took it.'

'There was something inside it which concerns only me,' I said. But I did not dare tell her what it was; she might think that the very same thing was of concern only to her. That's everything that happened.

She heard movement outside. 'I know now that they are searching for something which can be taken with them,' she said. 'I know, too, that it was I who brought them here. This is why you must not wake up, or else you will know that I have come to steal.'

She looked down at her lap. She rested her head, briefly, on her knee. 'I have told you everything,' she said. 'So please, don't wake up. I have done nothing wrong. It was her: she took the box, and I didn't dare ask her about it, so why are you coming to me now?'

She heard them running. 'Now everything is clear to you,' she said. 'And you must have known and chased after them. So don't go after me, then. I wanted only to tell you that I have been on a long journey. I thought the journey would be long, perhaps lasting until I came to you. I was always wanting to see you, but you came very early. There were many things scattered around my feet, and I could move only with great caution, so as not to touch any of the things. And this was very difficult indeed; so much so that I was forced to be afraid. And this fear I felt was very useful because it protected all the things. Yet in spite of that I was always making a mistake, because this whole matter was so very difficult.'

'I was hoping that you would wake up, now, and talk to me,' she said. 'If that were to happen, though, I know that you would chase me off and I would absolutely have to leave.'

She got to her feet. She left the room. She looked around. Shivered. Ran outside. Ran alongside the wall. She saw the policeman standing motionless. She saw the faint light in the old lantern flickering. She swerved with the wall. She felt afraid of the dark. She saw a faint light. She heard something moving. She leaned against the wall and gazed around cautiously.

'I must go back,' she said. She went back. She saw the dead body, lying on the floor of the empty room.

'I won't be able to take anything,' she said.

She left again. She walked with great caution. She ran. She saw them standing there. She was alarmed. She began running. They ran behind her.

'We took nothing,' they said. 'What did you take?'

'This,' she said. She extended her hand, closed into a fist. She opened her hand slowly. Her fingers separated and dangled in the air. The thing fell to the ground. They took it. They opened it.

'Does it concern you?' they asked.

'I don't know.'

'Does it concern us?'

'I don't know.'

'Whom does it concern?'

'Her, maybe. But when all is said and done, I really don't know.'

'The grey-haired woman was speaking,' she said. 'She said she hated that man very much, and at the very moment that she came to hate him so much he fell down dead. That's what she said.'

'Who will take this thing?' they asked.

'If we put it here,' she said, 'then perhaps he will come and take it, or she will, or someone, anyone, will come and take it.'

They put it down and went away. She stood there looking at it.

'I want it,' she said.

She left. She walked alongside the wall. She saw the dead body, lying on the empty pavement. She stopped. Looked at it.

'I left it behind,' she said. 'Maybe you need it.'

She was silent.

'Don't blame me,' she said. 'I left it for you. I'll bring it to you.'

She went back. But she didn't find it. She looked around; she saw the policeman standing on the other side, motionless.

'They put it right here,' she said, 'but it is no longer here.'

She went. She found the dead body, lying on the empty pavement. She pressed herself against the wall. She tried to run but could not.

'I left it behind,' she said. 'Perhaps you will take it. Why didn't you? They put many things - scattering them around - on the ground. Shall I bring them all to you? I am afraid to move my feet; they might brush against something. So I must move with care . . . therefore, I must not move at all. Shall I bring you all of them?'

And she said, 'All I really wanted was just to tell you that I was amazed when I realized that he was not at all friendly in his dealings with me. Maybe there was some reason for it, but I don't know what it could be. Maybe the reason was that he saw me losing the thing that you left for me. But I told you that I did not dare to ask her. Perhaps I really should go now, otherwise you might see me and take me away. I did tell you, after all, that you came very early.'

She walked. She heard a movement behind her. She was afraid, and ran over to the wall.

'I told you not to chase me,' she said. 'The wound was sunk deep into the forehead, and I had to feel afraid.'

She looked up. She collided with something and fell to the ground. She felt the edge of the pavement and found it sharp. She probed at her chest. She felt something sticky. She stretched her hand into the cavity. She saw the blood. She kissed it and soiled her face. She crawled. She turned over on her side. She looked at the dead body, cast down on the empty road.

'I had to feel afraid, always I had to. Thus, it was necessary that I not move at all. I told them not to put all of these things around my feet. It was very, very difficult.'

She stared off into the darkness. 'I didn't want you to come now,' she said. 'For will you, definitely, take me with you?'

NOTE
Title note: 'Tadi' al-ashya' al-mulqah 'ala al-tariq', published in *al-Karmil*, no. 14 (1984), pp. 77–8.

IN SEARCH OF A MAZE

Sahar Tawfiq

That evening, just like every evening, the thin, pale man with the strange fingers came and sat down on the same stone bench. His eyes stared at the same spot, their grey pupils circling and shifting within a small sphere, contemplating one and the same thing. He sat in solitude: hermitlike, distracted.

The first time she saw him, he exchanged a very few words with her, on the subject of music. He did not take notice of her again. It didn't appear that he knew her, nor did he exchange a single word with her.

Said came.

She got to her feet, joining him, and they left the place. They walked a little way and turned off towards the bridge. Nothing there but the river. Soon he began to talk. He spoke of many things: of his friends, his mother and father, of work and exhaustion and loneliness and the world, and of love. Only then did he tell her that he loved her, after he had told her all the first and rudimentary things, looking at her questioningly all the while.

When she did not respond, he asked, 'Aren't you going to say anything?'

But the river was alone there.

She told him then that talking about love was foolish, and futile in times like these.

She talked to him about herself.

She told him that her first relationship with a man had been bad. From the first day, she had known that it would end, but she hadn't resisted, until things reached a critical point. On that same day, she put an end to it all.

'I loved a man once,' she told him. 'And he loved me, and everything was lovely, it was really good, and there was nothing at all that could have interrupted it, nothing to raise any doubts.'

'Then what?' he asked her.

'Nothing.'

'Why did you leave him?'

'I didn't leave him.'

'He left you?'

'No, that didn't happen either.'

'Then, what did happen?'

'I don't know.'

She had sunk into gloom. She slowed down and her hand stiffened and contracted. They walked on in silence. Finally, she said that she wanted to go back.

Later she was sitting with her women friends. They were talking about the monster like a mermaid in reverse which had appeared in the Yemen. One of her friends was describing the mermaid's legs and knobbly knees, and then her body, and her head which resembled that of a fish. Then they talked about spirits and djinnis and told the latest anecdotes about them; they spoke of the most recent things they had done.

'Signs of the Day of Reckoning,' said one.

She wandered through some streets, very dark streets. She pondered on why she didn't believe these stories. She told herself that death was unbelievable, but that it happened. She didn't know what truth was and she felt afraid of the darkness.

Early in the morning she was sitting on the bank of the

Nile, a book between her hands. She began recalling the
first days of love. She had been young and impression-
able, and naïve, but everything had been fun and
beautiful. It was, in fact, a situation that she thought
could be likened to learning one's bearings, navigating
the ways of the city. At first, she had got lost frequently
while walking the streets of downtown Cairo. She'd
circle round and round, wandering all over, until she
came out into a place she knew.

Later on, she got to know one particular street well
and, whatever street she was on, she would head for that
one street. Still later, she became familiar with all the
streets and came to know them perfectly. Today, not a
byway or main street existed that she didn't know, but
often she would hope to get lost. Losing one's way was a
very good experience indeed, and a real pleasure,
especially since it was an ability that she had lost
entirely.

She thought of the mermaid which she found utterly
bewildering. The old man came. He sat down. He
appeared to her to be in another world, and it seemed
that long days had passed since she had last seen him.
His eyes were small and light-coloured. Whenever he
had come to mind, she hadn't been able to remember
the true colour of his eyes. She resolved that some day or
other she would follow him to wherever it was that he
came from.

He was clutching some papers through which he
began to riffle. She tried to focus her eyes on them but
she couldn't make out anything. Time passed as she
observed him and watched the skiffs and saw the Cairo
Tower, the Andalus Park and the motor cars on the
bridge.

Said came. They sat in silence. After a short while, the
old man arose from his place. She got to her feet.

'Where to?' asked Said.

'Come on, let's walk a little,' she said.

They walked.

'I brought you some sweets,' she said.

In a short while she began to laugh and joke, quickening her walk, sometimes so much that she was running. And then she would come to a stop, gazing at people and looking at the river and the trees. They sat down in a quiet place.

'What's wrong?' he asked her.

'Nothing.' After a pause, she said, 'I don't know, something will certainly happen, and when it does, everything will be clear.'

They walked on, in some tension. He walked her home and she went to bed and slept. That night, she dreamed that she was going out secretly to meet him, but some woman – or maybe it was a man – saw her, and then she hadn't known what to do. She had slapped him on the back and he had fallen over dead. She had felt very afraid, she had felt regret and confusion, she hid in a hollowed-out place so that no one would discover her. But they found her and took her away in a closed vehicle. It shot off at great speed as she wondered: why did this happen? and what are the real reasons behind it? But she couldn't think of any, and now she would be either hanged or imprisoned. She had no idea how she would endure either one. She felt that she had been treated unjustly and wronged limitlessly, and she thought she had done no wrong.

Finally, she awoke. She felt as if many things were being consumed by fire. She went out into the street, not knowing what to do. She imagined that if she saw him now she would throw herself into his embrace, and cry and cry, while he would gently pat her on the back. He would know everything and he wouldn't ask questions or blame her.

She went to Tahrir Square,* ascended the steps to the pedestrian bridge which encircled the vast roundabout, walked around it several times. She felt tired, and thought about sitting on the steps. She descended and walked to the corniche. The old man was sitting there, reading a small book.

She wished she could sit beside him and read with him. She longed for him to read to her in a calm and sympathetic voice, while she listened to him and gazed at the water, not saying a word.

After a time he got to his feet. She walked behind him. He took the bus, and so did she. He got off at one of the bus stops along the route, and she got out behind him. He crossed the square and turned off into a narrow street, then entered an area to which she had never been, one full of alleys, cul-de-sacs, and crowded, narrow streets. He went on, walking down one street, only to turn into another. Finally he came to an old house, its façade a faded yellow. Going down a few steps, he reached a doorway and went in. The interior was full of darkness.

She gazed for a while at the dark entryway before turning to go back. She discovered that she had forgotten the way she had come. She wandered through the small streets and alleys until she came out into the square.

She took a deep breath, filling her lungs, and gazed at the vast sky and the light encompassing the square at midday. She resumed walking, briskly now, smiling at everything and everybody. She looked at her watch; it was almost time for her appointment with Said. She found that it wasn't even particularly important to her. She stopped in a crowded spot, shading her eyes from the sun. At that moment, as her watch ticked on at its regular pace, she tried to recall the features of the old man. She tried very hard but she could not.

NOTES

Title note: 'Al-Bahth 'an mataha', published in the author's short-story collection *An tanhadira al-shams*, GEBO, Cairo 1985, pp. 59–65. Also in Edwar al-Kharrat (ed), *Mukhtarat: al-qissa al-qasira fi'l-sab'inat*,

Matbu'at al-Qahira, Cairo 1982, pp. 75-9.

Tahrir Square: 'Liberation Square', a main traffic roundabout and orientation point in downtown Cairo, named this after the 1952 revolution. It has recently been renamed Sadat Square, but is still known and referred to as Tahrir Square.